Book 2:
Fallout

Hayley Anderton & Laura Swift

.

Chapter One

Death wasn't like Fletcher had expected it to be.

He stirred. His eyes felt heavy and his limbs ached. But at least he could feel.

Is this heaven? Fletcher wondered. He'd never really been religious, so he hadn't had many thoughts on what came next after death...

But even he never thought that heaven would look like his high school cafeteria.

Slowly, Fletcher sat up, blinking in the bright daylight. His head swam and dark splotches lingered in his peripheral vision.

"Whoa, take it easy there, pal."

Fletcher jumped as a firm hand supported his back. He turned to see a friendly face peering at him. The face belonged to a young man, who had curly brown hair and blue eyes that looked at Fletcher with clear concern. He was dressed in blue nurses' scrubs that were splattered with dried blood.

Rather than push Fletcher back down - onto what he now realized was a stretcher - he helped prop Fletcher up gently against the wall of the cafeteria. Fletcher warmed to him right away, grateful for his help. Someone had draped a blanket over him, which he pulled up to his chin like a child.

"Are you feeling alright? You've had quite the week. Are you experiencing any symptoms?"

Fletcher rubbed at his temple, and then wished that he hadn't. He could feel the bruising on his hairline now, delicate and tender beneath his touch.

"Well...I'm a little dizzy...everything hurts...and I'm not sure whether this is all a hallucination or not."

The young man grinned. "I'd say all of that is natural, given what you've been through. I'm Patrick, by the way."

"Fletcher."

Patrick offered his hand for Fletcher to shake and he took it with a smile. It made him feel older than he was, like he was one of the adults.

"It's good to see you awake, Fletcher. You had a pretty nasty fall back there. Your head…"

Fletcher's fingers began to trace his hairline, more carefully this time. He felt a line of stitches running along the left side of his scalp. He winced at his own touch, his skin tender. He remembered being trapped in the classroom, the window his only means of escape. The black tarmac rising to meet him…

"Would you like to see?" Patrick asked him gently. Fletcher nodded and Patrick produced a mirror for Fletcher to examine himself in.

He was certainly looking a little worse for wear. His face blossomed with purple bruises. A ragged, raw set of stitches made him look like an old doll that had been hastily put back together. His white blonde hair was greasy and clung to his face with sweat.

So much for looking good on non-uniform day.

"You hit your head pretty hard when you fell."

"Did you see it happen?"

"No, but I heard the tale more than once." Patrick smiled sheepishly. "I can't lie, studying to be a nurse has made me a sucker for a gory story. I don't think we'd be talking now if you hadn't hit the edge of the roof before you hit the tarmac. I guess it slowed your fall a little. But still, it's lucky that Charlie and Nora found you when they did. We stitched you up best we could in the ambulance, but there might be some scarring…"

A sudden memory burst before Fletcher's eyes. Shouting, and the feeling of someone hoisting him off the ground and over their shoulder. The sound of feet pounding on tarmac as his head lolled like a pendulum. Then darkness, until now.

"I just don't understand…"

4

"It's okay. None of us do," Patrick said gently. "We got called to the school when it… happened. We were told that some students had been badly attacked by a teacher. We assumed that they'd had some kind of psychotic break. We weren't expecting…this. I'm training to be a nurse, but we had a staff shortage so they sent me along in the ambulance with the rest of the crew to help out. It was meant to be a learning experience, I guess." Patrick swallowed. "Well, we had to learn pretty fast. It was carnage here. Only Zoe and I are left now."

"But surely there's more help coming?" Fletcher asked, hopeful. But he knew, from the resignation in Patrick's face and the dark shadows under his eyes, that they were beyond helping.

"We've been trapped here for a week now, and nobody's come to help us."

"Wait, a *week*? I've been out of it for an entire *week*?"

"Well, in and out of it. But it's been a week since it all began, yes."

Fletcher felt his chest deflate. A week. A week, and those…*things* were still roaming the school hallways. *What if they roamed beyond the school hallways?* He shuddered.

What had happened to the world he once knew?

"The phones don't work," Patrick continued. "We theorized that there was a network update on the day everything went to shit, and it's knocked out communications. Or maybe an engineer turned when they were manning a telecom mast…I don't know. Tech isn't my forte. We tried the ambulance radios, and nobody answered at the other end. We even lost a few when we broke into the school office to try the computers…there was nothing."

Fletcher shook his head. He couldn't stop seeing the image of the undead forcing their way through the school, the very reason he had to jump in the first place. He shook his head a second time, as though trying to shake off his disbelief.

"What *are* those things?"

"The Zeds?"

"Zed for…?"

"…zombie? Yeah."

"Zombies." Fletcher let out a humorless laugh. "You've *got* to be kidding me. I didn't even get to finish high school…"

"Well, if you want some pointers for zombie school, here's a few we prepared earlier." Patrick cleared his throat. "Rule one; aim for the head. It's the only thing that stops them." He listed this off on his fingers. "Rule two; whatever you do, don't let them bite you."

"Rule three; no jumping out of windows," Fletcher added bitterly.

"You're a quick learner, Fletcher. Welcome to the team."

At the mention of 'team,' Fletcher took the opportunity to survey his high school cafeteria. With his head still throbbing, the rest of the room seemed muted until he really concentrated on his surroundings. Lunch tables were piled high against the double doors leading out to the corridor. A few lunch tables remained which students clustered around, playing cards or reading library books. Wooden vaulting boxes from gym class had been used to block the other set of doors that led to the outside recreation area. Javelins, rounders bats and fencing masks were piled in a corner; a haphazard makeshift amory against the Zeds.

Fletcher scanned the faces for anyone familiar. There was the kid from his English class who could quote Shakespeare by heart, and the guy from music who played the French horn in the school orchestra. Colin, Fletcher thought his name was.

But he couldn't see his sister.

"Hey, you haven't met a blonde girl called Cassie, have you?" Fletcher asked Patrick. The image of his sister running across the parking lot was vivid in his mind. She *had* been there. She'd come for him.

So why wasn't she here?

Patrick frowned. "It doesn't ring a bell…"

"She's my sister. I saw her, a few hours before I jumped, running across the parking lot…"

Patrick's smile sagged. Fletcher could tell that he was trying to muster some words of comfort, but it seemed to be a strain.

"Maybe it wasn't her," Patrick said gently.

Fletcher shook his head. He knew, in his gut, that he had seen Cassie. She had been his beacon of hope when he'd been locked alone in that room, waiting for something good to happen. But after a week, she could be anywhere.

After a week, she could already be dead.

"Ah, our sleeping beauty is awake!" trilled a bright female voice. The sound snapped Fletcher from his morbid thoughts. A young woman, Fletcher guessed the same age as Patrick, was walking towards them across the cafeteria. Her long brown hair was pulled into a ponytail away from her face, and she had large brown eyes that were filled with warmth. She, too, was dressed in nurses' scrubs, although they were somewhat cleaner than Patrick's. She was very pretty, with flawless skin that glowed and the longest eyelashes that Fletcher had ever seen.

But most importantly, she was holding a tray of food. Fletcher's stomach growled in anticipation.

She peered down at Fletcher as she placed the food tray beside him.

"You look terrible!" Zoe said, but not unkindly.

"Cut him some slack Zo, he's just woken up," Patrick said. "We can't *all* look as great as you…"

"I'd look a lot worse if those Zeds had got me," Fletcher pointed out. The new word felt foreign in his mouth.

"Saying you look better than a Zed isn't saying much," Patrick joked. Fletcher felt himself warming to the pair immediately. There was a tenderness in how Patrick looked at Zoe, and Fletcher sensed something between them. Something sweet, something pure, in a world filled with darkness.

7

"Good to know he's been caught up with our slang," Zoe said to Patrick fondly, resting a hand on his shoulder. She turned to Fletcher. "Zed was Patrick's suggestion. He's very proud of it."

"Better than your suggestion of 'munchers', don't you think?" Patrick grumbled.

Zoe chose to ignore Patrick, aiming her bright smile at Fletcher instead. "How are you feeling?"

"Like I've jumped out a window and had my head sewn back together?"

"About right," Zoe said. She smiled at Fletcher and gestured to the tray. "Well go on, you must be starving."

Ravenous, Fletcher wolfed down the sandwich Zoe had prepared for him. He popped open the can of lemonade and glugged it down thirstily. He reached for the apple next, taking a large bite. He was grateful for the food, even if it was, Fletcher shuddered to think, *healthy*.

"At least we didn't need to worry about your appetite," Patrick chuckled.

"So how did this all start?" Fletcher asked between mouthfuls. He gestured to the cafeteria.

"People just sort of naturally gravitated here," Zoe said. "Out of habit I guess, they saw it as a place of safety. Or a meeting point, maybe. A few students - Charlie and Nora, mainly - grabbed the javelins and bats from the gym before they trapped a load of Zeds in there. We've been holed up here ever since."

"We wouldn't want to get stuck in a classroom either," Patrick added. "We found a group trapped in the library, with no food and no way of escape…they'd have been screwed if we hadn't turned up. At least here, we're close to the food, and there's not just one exit."

"Doesn't that make it harder to defend?"

"We've been lucky so far," Patrick replied grimly.

"So you haven't left the school?"

Zoe shook her head. "We thought help would come."

Of course they did. Fletcher had never thought, when he was being chased down the corridor by those snarling creatures, that it was something he'd have to live with. It was just a nightmare he was sure would end with him waking up, safe and sound. But seeing the small number of students and the ways in which they'd adapted to survive felt like a stark awakening.

This was the world now. And Fletcher would have to do whatever it took to survive.

"People are scared," Patrick added. "They're mostly kids. Some of them haven't even been away from their parents for this long before."

"We've got plenty of food…" Zoe chimed up, as though to brighten the dark scenario. Then her face fell. "Although I suppose that it will run out eventually…"

Fletcher looked guiltily at the crumbs on his tray.

"Charlie and Nora are back!" one of the students shouted from across the cafeteria. A few students, including the two Fletcher recognised, shifted the gym vaulting box out of the way of one of the doors. Two tall figures slipped through the gap in the door, panting.

Patrick helped Fletcher to his feet, and Fletcher followed him and Zoe tentatively over to sit on a spare table. He wrapped the blanket around his shoulders, out of comfort more than the cold. He watched Charlie and Nora help the other students quickly replace the barricade, sealing off the cafetera.

Charlie was tall, with an athletic build and handsome features. His skin was dark and his black hair was shaved close to his scalp. Nora by contrast was pale, slightly shorter than her companion, with black curled hair piled on top of her head in a tight bun. They were both armed with kitchen knives.

And they were covered in blood.

Fletcher watched the pair move through the room, checking in with all the students dotted about the room. Despite looking slightly younger than Patrick and Zoe, Fletcher got the impression that the mismatched group of survivors looked to Charlie and Nora as leaders. They walked in with an air of authority and Fletcher had almost felt a collective sigh of relief from the other students when they had entered.

After greeting all the students, Charlie and Nora headed over to the table where Patrick, Zoe and Fletcher were sitting.

"He's awake!" Zoe said excitedly as they headed over.

Smiles replaced their grim expressions. They slid down into seats on the other side of the table, knives clattering on the wooden surface.

"Nice of you to finally join us," Charlie joked. He had an easy smile that crinkled the corners of his dark eyes. "I'm Charlie, and this is Nora."

"Fletcher."

"I'd shake your hand but…" Charlie shrugged, looking at the scarlet that stained his hands.

"They saved you from the Zeds that first day," Zoe explained.

"Thank you," Fletcher said. "All of you. For everything."

"It's getting worse out there," Nora said, addressing Patrick and Zoe whilst chewing gum. "We thought we'd contained most of the Zeds to the corridors downstairs, but they keep finding a way up. They're getting through barricades faster than we can put them up."

"What about the ground floors?" Fletcher asked. The high school spanned four floors; a basement, ground floor, first floor and second floor. The cafeteria was on the first floor.

"Think about a sandwich," Nora said, popping her pink bubblegum. "Zeds, us, Zeds." She demonstrated with her hands and Fletcher noticed her long acrylic nails were stained red. "We're in the middle of a shit sandwich."

Fletcher hadn't realized it before, but whilst the cafeteria was quiet, there was a steady hum of background noise.

A noise that sounded an awful lot like the moan of hungry mouths.

"We've cleared the floor," Charlie said. "There were only five yesterday, but we got rid of about ten today?" He looked to Nora for confirmation, who nodded.

"So, what are you saying?" Patrick asked.

"I don't know if it makes sense to stay," Nora continued quietly. "The longer we stay in here, the worse it gets. And the longer we stay in here, the more scared people will be of what's out *there*. Charlie and I can do all the patrols we like, but we just don't have the numbers to clear the entire school of Zeds. Or defend it, even if we could clear it. We're in a ticking time bomb."

"It's been a week now, and nobody has been to rescue us," Charlie said. "We can keep people safe, but it feels like preventing the inevitable. I can't speak for you all, but I think the best chance of survival is to get the hell out of here. We can't stay here forever."

Fletcher got the impression that the pair had already prepared this discussion. From the unsurprised looks on Patrick and Zoe's faces, this wasn't news to them either.

"We don't really know what's out there," Patrick said. "But there *have* to be other survivors."

"Then let's find them," Fletcher piped up at last. The others turned to him. He swallowed nervously, not wanting to intrude whilst voicing his opinions. "My sister is out there; there will be others too."

Charlie nodded his agreement. "The others look to us as leaders," he said, gesturing to himself, Nora, Patrick and Zoe. "We need to encourage them to come with us."

Nora sighed. "We're not babysitters," she argued. "I'm not risking my life for some kid who's scared of the dark."

"Nora - "

11

"We are the *only* ones who patrol, Charlie. Other than using the toilets, they've all stayed in here. How is it going to be any different out there?" She gestured to the windows, where clear blue skies teased them invitingly. "If anything, it's going to be worse. And none of them are prepared for it."

Fletcher sensed that they'd already had this argument too.

"If we leave, we open the door to anyone else who wants to come along," Zoe established firmly. There was conviction in her expression that told them not to argue otherwise. "We can't drag people along, but we can't just leave them to fend for themselves."

"But they have to be prepared to fight," Charlie added swiftly, sensing Nora's distaste.

"We could just do a run, for now," Patrick suggested. "See what's beyond the school gates before we start causing panic? Maybe take a few of the older kids and get them prepared."

"So it's settled. Tomorrow, we see what's out there," Nora said pushily.

"That sounds sensible," Zoe agreed. "I know you two have seen the state of the rest of the school, but none of us knows what's beyond here."

"God help us if it's worse than here," Charlie mumbled, putting his head in his hands. "Or we're doomed."

Chapter Two

Warren trudged across the yard, his hands dug deep into his pockets to keep the cold from nipping his fingers. The day was only just beginning, and the skies were still dark. When Ginge had told him that he'd have to be up early to help her on the farm, he hadn't quite expected to be up before the sun, but he wasn't about to start complaining now.

The one thing he hated most was walking through the farm alone. Ginge, used to the early mornings, had gone on ahead to get started, but that meant Warren had to take the short walk over the bridge to the barns without her. His heart was thudding so hard against his chest that he felt sick. He barely dared to blink, scared that he'd miss the moment a rotter appeared and sunk its teeth into him…

Warren shuddered at the thought. He still couldn't get used to the new world that they were living in. He'd barely slept all week since arriving at the farm. He was surrounded by strange people that he barely knew. He'd been thrown into new tasks that he had no idea how to complete. And every now and then, he was forced to get his hands dirty and kill something that once used to be human.

Just the average coming-of-age experience, Warren thought to himself.

But he couldn't deny that one good thing had come out of the entire thing. As he neared the barns, he could see Ginge, wrapped up in her big coat with beautiful red hair spilling out over her shoulders. He smiled to himself, glad she hadn't spotted him yet. It gave him a moment to admire her from afar. He'd been drawn to her since the day he arrived. She was his beacon of brightness among the dreariness of day to day life. He could barely believe he'd never noticed her at college before. Their college was a big place, he supposed, but he knew if they were ever to return there, he'd be looking for her in the crowd. He could almost imagine waiting outside class for her, walking her to the cafeteria, fetching her tea from the canteen…

But that wasn't going to happen. Warren was starting to grasp that, now. If help never came, then this was going to be their life. Him, waking up at the crack of dawn every day to help on the farm. Her, leading the group through their hardships like a guiding light.

Them, spending every day together for as long as they could stay alive.

Ginge looked up as Warren trudged closer to the barns. She caught his eye and he managed a shy, sleepy smile in return. She was petting the head of one of the cows gently as they mooed collectively, a somber sound that Warren was starting to get used to. They were penned in by a metal gate, which Ginge clambered over easily as he approached.

"Time to scoop some poop," Ginge said brightly, nodding to two shovels by the gate. "Pass me one, would you?"

Warren did so. He was still too shy to say much around Ginge, but she didn't seem to mind. He always did what she asked of him, so that made him a good team mate to have out there. Plus, he didn't mind getting his hands dirty.

It took almost an hour for the pair of them to clean out the cow shed together, maneuvering their way around the cows delicately as they went about their own morning routine. By the time they'd finished up and the daylight was breaking, Warren felt his muscles aching and his tired eyes drooping, but it felt good to be doing labor. It felt good to be useful.

Ginge allowed them to rest for a moment, leaning against her shovel as she surveyed the animals in front of her.

"I don't know how we're going to keep on top of everything," she admitted. "We're used to having more help around here. And with no more feed coming in…they'll run out of food. I suppose I could clear out one of the fields, let them roam free and graze…but I'm scared of a horde coming and hurting them. Even then, it wouldn't be enough. Not to last all winter."

Warren didn't often hear Ginge voice her worries. She usually just knuckled down and got on with the task in front of her. He didn't envy her position. Since her parents were gone now, Ginge had become the de facto leader of the place, and that meant responsibility that shouldn't rest on the shoulders of any seventeen year old.

"Whatever you need, I can help you," Warren told her. Ginge looked at him then, her blue eyes dulled by tiredness.

"You know, I really appreciate that," she said softly. "Everyone's doing their bit around here…I know that. But you're the only one who has stepped up on the farm." She smiled to herself. "Not that I ever expected Cara to get involved, even if she grew up here. And who were my other options? Luke is too busy playing the military commander, and Poppy's probably scared of ruining her new jeans or something."

Warren smiled. "I'm not sure that's completely fair. Cassie did persuade Poppy to help her take the bins out the other day."

Ginge laughed. It was a beautiful sound, one that echoed through the quiet morning air. Seemingly surprised at the outburst, Ginge clasped a hand to her own mouth. They'd noticed that the rotters seemed sensitive to noise, and the sound from the barns was already drawing them in too close for comfort every day. They lived in constant fear of bringing them too close.

But Warren thought it was worth the risk to hear such a lovely sound. They didn't have much to laugh about those days. Laughter was one of those rare moments that shouldn't feel special, and yet it did.

Ginge composed herself, glancing around suspiciously as though expecting a horde of rotters to materialize. It was back to reality for them. Warren had managed to forget for a moment where they were. But now, his feet were firmly back on the ground.

"Anyway," Ginge said, her voice lower now, almost a whisper. "Maybe I'm just tired and moody and finding flaws in everyone. I mean, these are my friends and I love them. But I do wish I had some extra helping hands out here. I'm trying to keep things running. And I know that they're all taking it in turns on watch, but there are other things to do." Ginge paused, glancing at Warren with a guilty look in her eyes. "Sorry. I don't make a habit of talking behind people's backs. I guess…sometimes it feels a bit lonely. Lonely and tiring and frustrating. Like I'm constantly shouting into the void."

"You're not shouting into the void. I'm listening," Warren said softly. Ginge's eyes locked on to his and for a moment, they watched one another carefully.

"I know that," Ginge whispered back. Then, she tore her gaze from his, propping her shovel up against the wall. "Alright. Lots to do…and it looks like it's going to start raining soon. Cara promised she'd take the kids to check on the hens and hopefully collect some eggs…so do you want to help me milk the dairy cows?"

Warren wavered. "What if I hurt them?"

Ginge tutted. "You're not going to hurt them. Not when I'm teaching you what to do. Come on, or you're failing Ginge's farming school!"

Warren smiled and followed her through the yard without protest. He'd follow her anywhere.

Cassie trudged outside with two mugs of hot tea in her hand. She had borrowed one of Ginge's raincoats and it was pulled up over her head to protect her from the relentless drizzle. Poppy was already sitting on the deckchair outside, keeping watch with her knees drawn up to her chest. It was miserable keeping watch at the best of times, but it was even worse in the rain.

"Here's your tea," Cassie said to Poppy, handing her a mug. "Drink it quick, though, before the rain waters it down."

Poppy took a half-hearted sip of the warm drink, clearly trying not to wince. "No milk?"

Cassie shook her head. They'd run out two days previously, and it had made the prospect of a cup of tea seem less comforting. Particularly since they were using every tea bag twice to save on supplies, an idea introduced by Luke. He ran a tight ship on their inventory, among other things.

"Are you sure that Luke isn't hiding it somewhere as rations?" Poppy asked bitterly. Droplets of water ran down her forehead. "This isn't wartime. This can't last much longer...can it?"

Cassie said nothing. She didn't want to be the bearer of bad news. All around her, she could see that it was sinking in to her friends that they were on their own. No one was coming to save them. But for whatever reason, Poppy had fallen behind in that aspect. It was like she couldn't face the idea of what was to come.

And who could blame her?

"You know what I was thinking about this morning?" Cassie said, trying to divert the conversation. "Camping. When I was pulling on my wellies I just thought of all those wet, rainy mornings we used to spend camping out in one another's gardens...or when I went camping with Heidi and Eliza and our entire tent flooded. Everything was wet, and there's no relief when you get out of the tent, either. There's nowhere else to go. It's just endless sogginess. That's what it feels like when we come and sit out here."

"Except there's no s'mores or singing around the campfire whilst you and Eliza play guitar," Poppy said, her chin resting on her knees. She glanced sideways at Cassie. "I know what you're trying to do. You're trying to distract me from it all. And I appreciate that. But how can I ignore it? We're sitting out here, waiting for rotters to show up. It scares me, and I want out. But I'm choosing to believe that someone is going to help us soon. That's what keeps me going."

"Okay," Cassie said gently. "Okay."

Poppy sighed. "I know maybe I'm being naive. But trying to imagine this as our future…it's unbearable for me. I'm not cut out for it. Not like the rest of you."

"Don't say that. You held your own back at college…"

"That was different. I was forced to. And I guess instinct kicked in. But it's different here. You see them coming from a mile off. You're forced to prepare yourself for what you're about to do. To kill something…someone. Someone that used to be like us." Poppy shook her head to herself, as though trying to shake away the bad thoughts. "It's too much for me. I don't want to fight. I don't want this kind of life. But…but I also don't want to end up like Gemma. Like Rob. One of them."

Cassie's stomach churned. In her dreams every night, she saw Rob's face after he had turned. She heard the sound of Toby being torn apart, of Gemma's screams echoing through the night. She'd never forget those things for as long as she lived. Even if the world went back to the way it was, she'd still have the echoes of those memories to live with forever, like a recurring nightmare you just can't shift. She'd always know those memories were true.

And then there were the things she didn't know. Things that scared her, hurt her. The question of whether her parents were alive out there somewhere. The question of whether Fletcher had managed to hold his own at the school. Was *anything* left out there? None of them had left the farm since they'd arrived a week before. They had no way of contacting anyone, and there was no way of knowing if they were the very last people on Earth or not. Sometimes it felt like they must be, alone in the countryside with not another human in sight.

At least, not any living ones.

Cassie reached out silently for Poppy's hand. Poppy didn't raise her head, but she squeezed Cassie's hand in return, both of them silently coming to terms with everything they were still yet to face. Everything was uncertain, everything was terrifying.

But at least they had one another.

"I've already told you, it's a no," Luke said, trying to ignore Heidi as he read over his notes. He was sitting at the kitchen table, observing the plans he'd drawn up for the farm. He'd been busy in the last week, figuring out how best to defend the farm, how to ration their supplies, and how to keep them all alive. Unfortunately for him, it seemed that everyone else was determined to derail his plans.

"I wasn't asking for your permission. I was telling you that we're doing it," Heidi said, perching on the edge of the kitchen table. She was holding her trusty screwdriver in one hand. Toby's penknife peeked out from her jeans pocket. "We can't just stay here forever, can we, waiting for things to blow over? So it's time we left the farm for the first time. We're going to need to go and grab some supplies from the shops before they run out."

"This isn't Supermarket Sweep," Luke snapped. "You think you're just going to stroll into Tesco and grab whatever you fancy? Everyone is going to have the same idea. And a lot of those people are going to get themselves killed in the process. That means a build up of rotters in areas of interest. And *that* is why it's not a good idea."

Heidi raised an eyebrow. "I bet you're going to think differently when we run out of toilet roll. Besides, we ran out of cookies on the first day, and I'm getting hangry."

"Haven't you ever heard of living off the land?" Luke muttered, still refusing to look at Heidi. "We're lucky that we're somewhere that doesn't require us to scavenge and get ourselves killed. Once we pasteurize the milk and the crops come through, we'll be just fine."

"You know that's not going to be enough," Heidi said. "Anything can happen." She hopped down from atop the table and headed to the kitchen cupboards, opening them for dramatic flair. Most of them were half-full, but she shook her head. Ginge had a bigger family than most so she'd been well stocked, but even her cupboards were quickly emptying out. Almost as though they hadn't bothered to prepare for the apocalypse at all...

"We have a lot of mouths to feed. This stuff is only going to last us so long. And in case you haven't noticed, winter is on its way. The crops you're talking about aren't going to come for months. And then, when the rest of the food runs out too, everyone else will have raided the good stuff." She paused, letting that sink in. "Did I mention that we're out of cookies?"

"If I hear you mention cookies one more time..."

"Cookies?" Rori said, popping his head around the kitchen door. Luke heaved a sigh. In terms of pains in his butt, Heidi and Rori were beginning to come as a pair, a double pronged annoyance.

"I suppose you're supporting her nonsense too?"

Rori chewed his thumb. "I don't know. I mean, personally I have no desire to go out there. I don't feel safe here, let alone in unknown territory. But you're the one who keeps talking about the long term. If this is life now, don't we have to take some risks to keep ourselves safe in the future?"

Luke tapped his pen against his chin. He glanced over at Heidi. "You see, he made a much more convincing and articulate argument than you did."

Heidi shrugged. "Still means I'm right. And hey, since you're so keen on *living off the land,* maybe we can swing by the garden center up the road. I doubt people will think to look there, and there might be some stuff we can make use of on the farm."

"Alright. I guess it's not the dumbest thing you've ever suggested. Well, if you can find someone crazy enough to go with you, then be my guest."

Rori and Heidi exchanged a glance. Rori raised a hesitant, but wide smile.

"I'll go if you go."

Heidi grinned back. "You're making me seem like a bad influence. Come on. Let's go rally some troops. We move at first light!"

Heidi and Rori left the room together, thick as thieves. Luke muttered under his breath, turning back to his plans in disapproval. Some part of him knew that they had to explore beyond the borders of the farm. But, with his ankle still throbbing from his fall back at the college, the thought of leaving the farm was a scary one. What if they weren't as lucky as they had been on the day it all began? Luke knew how fortunate they'd been to make it out of the college alive. What if they returned empty handed and with less people than they began with? He thought of the names that were etched onto the tree in the yard. He didn't want his own name to end up there. And, annoying as they were, he didn't want to see Heidi or Rori's names there, either.

He didn't want to see any more deaths.

"Oh, and Luke?" Heidi sang, popping her head back around the door.

Luke put down his pen with a pointed sigh. "What?"

"We're going to need you to drive."

Chapter Three

Cook dinner. That was the instruction Zoe had left for Fletcher and Patrick before slipping through the cafeteria's barricade in the direction of the gym showers. Fletcher and Patrick stood in the refrigerator light, weighing up their options.

"You're a student, surely you know how to cook?" Fletcher said.

Patrick blushed. "If you call instant noodles cooking, sure." He reached into the fridge for a packet of something green that looked to Fletcher like it was too healthy to taste nice. "But I don't know what to do with an asparagus…"

Fletcher wrinkled his nose. "Asparagus soup?"

"Do you know *how* to make soup?"

"Good point." Fletcher thought back to the school lunches that were usually on offer. Chicken burgers, paninis, salads, pasta, pizza slices…there was always a ripple of excitement through the student body at the prospect of chips on a Friday. Fletcher wondered if he'd ever experience that kind of naive joy again.

Patrick searched through the fridge. "We've got chicken breasts, some garlic bread…"

"Sounds like my sort of food."

"There's chips in the freezer…"

They'd already run out of ice cream and all of the varieties of cake that the dinner ladies had baked. With no adults to tell them what they could and couldn't eat, the students had turned to easy comfort foods. Chicken nuggets, pizza slices and sandwiches were the most popular choices. Despite Zoe's push to eat fresh fruit and vegetables, they had been mostly left forgotten for tastier treats, and that meant Fletcher had mostly missed out on the best foods during his unconsciousness. Now, his stomach growled at the thought of what was to come

Fletcher busied himself slicing bread buns whilst Patrick put a tray of frozen chips into the huge kitchen oven. Patrick hummed to himself as he made preparations, making Fletcher smile. He saw Patrick as a cool older brother, someone he looked up to, but who was still young at heart. The pair had got on instantly, and Fletcher was grateful as the day wore on that he wasn't alone in this. Patrick and Zoe were the reason he was alive, and he owed them big time.

"What's the goriest thing you've ever seen?" Fletcher asked Patrick eagerly. He was fascinated by Patrick's experience as a student nurse.

"What, aside from everything the Zeds have done?" Patrick considered this. "I get to steer clear of some of the goriest stuff since I'm still a student. But I've seen some hellish things. Maggots in wounds, pus galore...." Patrick's eyes lit up mischievously. "Oh, you'll like this one. I saw a motorcyclist once in A&E who'd degloved his foot. That was pretty grim."

"Degloved?"

"It's when friction causes skin and soft tissue to get ripped from the body." Patrick held up a cheese grater to demonstrate. "Imagine rubbing up against this really quickly."

Fletcher wrinkled his nose in disgust. "Urgh...wicked."

"Not for him; he needed a couple of skin grafts. It didn't put him off motorbiking, though."

"Is it different, seeing the Zeds compared to patients?" Fletcher asked.

Patrick thought about this. "I guess it's hard," he admitted. "My instinct is to help. I see a bite and mentally run through the steps for how I'd treat it. The nurse in me wants to patch those poor souls up. That's why I don't tend to go out there much." He nodded his head toward the nearer set of double doors. "But they don't seem to be in pain, which helps dissociate the person from the monster. As someone gets older, they can lose their memories, their awareness, even a sense of who they are. But pain is the one constant that remains. They don't feel pain, and that makes it easier for me not to feel the pull to help them. But I also know that there's nothing left of the person anymore if they can't feel pain. It's easier, and it's harder. Does that make sense?"

Fletcher nodded. "What do you think it is? What do you think makes them Zeds?"

"It's a parasite, I think," Patrick mused. "But a parasite that feeds off a host - in this case, us - killing until it completely inhabits and controls the physical body and all its functions. Viruses don't *want* to kill a host; they need the host to spread the virus. That's the bit I can't figure out. Someone smarter than me will be working on a theory, I suppose."

"Do you think they're dead, then?"

Patrick paused. "I do," he said quietly. "Or at least, I hope so."

They served up the food they'd cooked in a companionable silence, Fletcher mulling over Patrick's words. He remembered learning about the common cold in biology class; how it mutated year on year and rippled through the student body at the start of each semester. If the virus, or parasite, or whatever it was, could turn people into animated corpses…then what might it do next?

He was pulled from his thoughts when Zoe returned from her shower, hair piled up into a towel wrapped around her head. She approached the boys eagerly.

"Dinner is served," Fletcher announced proudly.

He caught a glimmer of disappointment on Zoe's face as the lights flickered, before cutting out completely and plunging them into darkness.

Then the screams started.

"What do you miss most? About normality, I mean?" Charlie asked.

Charlie and Nora were doing their evening patrol, making sure the floor was clear of Zeds. Mostly, Nora found the experience to be a chore, but it was necessary to give the others a sense of security. Most of the younger students wouldn't use the bathrooms until they knew that Charlie and Nora had given the all-clear. In the first days, a few of them had even chosen to wet themselves out of fear of leaving the cafeteria. Charlie himself had been found in a compromising position, having fought off a Zed that snuck up on him in the toilets. Hearing the commotion, Nora had been greeted by the sight of Charlie with his pants around his ankles in a cubicle and a Zed motionless between them.

"Well, my my, that *is* distracting," Nora had smirked, biting her tongue as she eyed Charlie's physique. Charlie had squirmed, quickly trying to regain his modesty. But then again, there were never truly any secrets between him and Nora.

"I miss Drive Thru's the most," Nora said. "This is the longest I've been without an iced coffee, like, *ever*."

"That explains why you're always so grouchy."

"... and why I find you so annoying," Nora said sweetly.

"It's character developing, you know, surviving coffee withdrawal."

"If I develop any more, I am going to develop into a villain," Nora threatened.

"You don't see yourself as the leading lady? Shocking," Charlie said with a raised eyebrow. "I can see our story unfolding…we could be like the Bonnie and Clyde of the zombie apocalypse…but instead of robbing banks, we steal instant coffee from those who cross our path."

Nora snorted. "I'm a caffeine addict, not an outlaw Charlie."

"I'm struggling to see the difference…"

"But Bonnie and Clyde were a couple," Nora mused, ignoring him. "That's what makes them so dynamic. They're a power couple."

"We're *basically* a power couple," Charlie said.

"Just without the couple element…"

"Are you telling me that you don't find all *this-*" he gestured to the dried blood that had crusted on the floor, and the crumpled bodies of Zeds, "terribly romantic? Jeez, I make all this effort, bring you to these nice places…"

Nora smiled to herself, turning her face away from Charlie. It wasn't as if the thought of being with him hadn't crossed Nora's mind. But they were so different. Charlie was liked by everyone, and Nora was admired. It was a distinction that seemed important to Nora.

Still, the heart wants what it wants, Nora thought. They'd almost hooked up a few times in the past, back when their teenage lives had revolved around socials and football games.

But it seemed there was nothing like a zombie apocalypse to get her hormones truly racing.

"You sure know how to charm a girl, Charlie. Flowers and chocolate are *so* overrated these days."

"Wait… so I'm not getting flowers *or* chocolate?"

Nora shoved him playfully, almost skipping in front of him. "You wish."

"At least tell me I look pretty," Charlie called at her retreating back. "Flip the switch, Nora. Girls don't need to wait around for guys to make a move anymore…"

Nora glanced over her shoulder and saw horror dawn on Charlie's face. She knew she was in trouble before she felt the rotting hands clamp down on her shoulder.

She swung around, trying to free herself from its tightening grasp. She heard a hungry snarl emit from ruined lips that were too close to the bare skin of her neck. Her heart pounded as she tried to wriggle free from its hold.

Charlie dragged the Zed away from Nora by its hood, pushing it away from them before smashing his baseball bat over its head. It crumpled to the floor.

Charlie caught Nora's eye. A pause hung between them. Then they were on each other, almost wrestling as their lips met and Charlie slid his hands around Nora's waist. Their lips were hot and they were breathless. There was so much risk in the moment, but it only seemed to make the kiss that much sweeter.

Nora pulled away to gauge his reaction. The smile on his face was the last thing Nora saw before they were plunged into darkness.

"So the lights went out on your floor too?" Patrick asked.

On their return, Charlie and Nora had re-grouped with Fletcher, Patrick and Zoe in the kitchen. Fear was contagious, and panic had rippled among the other students when the lights in the cafeteria had cut out. Zoe had found some matches and a few candles in the kitchen, some of which were lit now. The flames cast flickering shadows over the walls, illuminating the fear on all the faces around the room.

It was Colin, the French horn player, who had surprisingly stepped up to keep everyone calm. Small and skinny for his age, with thick round glasses and a mop of messy ginger hair, he didn't look like the sort to lead the herd. But he'd distracted his terror-stricken peers with the food that Fletcher and Patrick had cooked. The others were grateful for the time to discuss tactics privately, and Fletcher felt proud that he was included in the conversation.

Charlie nodded. "Every single one. We're lucky to make it back in one piece really. I literally thought I was going to have to make a stab in the dark."

"I think it's safe to assume that means all the electricity is out," Zoe reasoned. She'd already checked all the kitchen appliances. Their digital screens had stared back blankly. "For every floor."

"There's got to be *some* sort of backup electrical system though," Patrick thought out loud. "We have them in the hospital. Sure, keeping life-saving equipment going is slightly different to powering a school, but you'd think there would be something, at least."

"There are backup generators in the basement," Charlie said grimly. "In the caretaker's office. I went down there at the start of all of this, thinking it would be safer, but that's where most of the Zeds are now."

"We want to leave anyway," Nora pointed out. "Who cares if we get the lights back on? Let's just go now. What do we have to lose?"

"We don't know what's out there yet," Zoe reasoned. "It could be worse than here. It's not just lights, it's food too. The freezers are stocked. We can't let that go to waste. If we stay, we'll need it. Or someone will." She looked at the group huddled around the flickering candle. "We can't leave them with nothing."

"The backup generators won't last forever," Nora argued. "Nor will frozen hash browns and pizza slices. They'll realize that the hard way if they stay."

"What Nora's saying," Charlie swiftly interjected. "Is that it's us who will be risking our lives to get the generators running. That's a big risk if we aren't staying."

"But we might need to stay," Patrick reminded them quietly. "At least, for now. We can't run the risk of wasting whatever food we have."

Charlie looked at Nora. "They do have a point," he admitted.

"But we're only two hands against a bunch of Zeds," Nora protested shrilly. "In the *dark*."

"I'll come with you," Fletcher said suddenly, surprising even himself. He saw the skeptical look that Patrick and Zoe shared. "I'm fine," he reassured them. "I want to help. I wouldn't be alive without you...all of you. Let me help. I owe you."

"It's a free country. If you feel up to it, we can't say no," Charlie said. He clapped Fletcher on the back. It made Fletcher feel important, like he was one of the crew. He was respected.

"We could use the extra hands," Nora admitted, realizing she was defeated. "Thanks, Fletch."

Fletch. That was what his family called him. The familiar nickname sounded bittersweet from a stranger's mouth. But maybe this was his mismatched family now. After all, all they had was each other.

"But if I die turning some lights on, I will come back to haunt you all," Nora warned.

Fletcher slipped through the doors after Charlie and Nora. A thin square of weak light shone on the empty stairwell below them. Looking behind him, Patrick and Zoe squinted after them through the glass in the door.

Good luck, Patrick mouthed. Fletcher nodded at him, willing himself to look brave. But now he was outside of the safety of the cafeteria, he didn't feel brave at all. His breath rattled behind the fencing mask he wore for protection, but it was too big and it kept slipping down his face. The hand clutching his javelin was slick with sweat, and his skinny knees were trembling.

"We don't want you getting too close to them," Charlie had said when he'd handed Fletcher the weapon. "Nora and I will lead the way. We just need you to watch our backs and handle any stragglers heading for the stairwell."

The message was clear. Stick to the back and only attack from a safe distance. But still, when nobody was watching, Fletcher had slipped a knife from the kitchens into the back pocket of his jeans.

He only hoped he wouldn't need it.

"You okay, Fletch?" Nora asked when the trio reached the bottom of the stairwell. There was a kindness in her voice that Fletcher hadn't heard before. He sensed her tough exterior was a facade, a way to keep others at bay.

"Let's get this over with," Fletcher replied. It had sounded much cooler in his head, but it came out shaky and desperate. His mouth was dry and his hands were clammy. He was glad that the darkness concealed his nerves, but it only amplified the scariness of the situation.

Charlie fumbled with the handles of the double doors, which were tied shut with electrical charging cables. Once the cables were free, Charlie eased the doors open just wide enough for someone to slip through.

"See you on the other side," Nora said. She winked at Fletcher before she disappeared into the dark corridor beyond. Fletcher watched the darkness swallow Charlie too, until he was alone in the stairwell.

Fletcher slithered into the gap between the doors. The emergency Fire Exit sign cast an eerie green glow over the corridor. Fletcher felt his trainer slide in something slick on the smooth floor. He ignored the urge to check what it was, already knowing the answer.

He padded cautiously down the hallway. He could just make out the dark outlines of Charlie and Nora ahead of him in the gloom. It was the sort of darkness that pressed on Fletcher's eyes, suffocating his sight. He strained his ears for any sign of danger. Charlie and Nora moved through the corridor soundlessly with well-practiced stealth.

They turned a corner and met their first Zed. It ambled towards Nora with hungry moans, but she dispatched it swiftly and quietly with a swing of her baseball bat. It crumpled to the floor, and Fletcher stepped over the body cautiously as they continued.

Charlie paused outside a door that had a plaque on it. Fletcher couldn't quite make out the writing in the dark, but he assumed it was the caretaker's office. Confirming his suspicions, Charlie eased the door open. It swung forwards silently, and Charlie paused. Hearing nothing, he stepped into the office carefully, leaving Nora and Fletcher outside.

From nowhere, a dark shape lumbered toward Charlie. It grabbed the hood of his jacket and Charlie stumbled, losing his balance. The two figures crashed into the wooden shelving unit, where hammers, brushes and various other tools rained down on top of them.

Frozen in fear, Fletcher watched Charlie grab a hammer and swing it through the air into the Zed's temple with a sickening crunch. The Zed toppled backwards as Charlie wrenched the hammer free.

The clang of a mop falling on a metal bucket signaled the end of the attack.

There was a pause, their eyes glinting in the darkness as the three of them looked at each other in horror. The sound of hungry, snarling mouths met their ears. The sound had been almost like ringing the dinner bell for the Zeds.

They were coming.

"Charlie - the generator - now!" Nora cried.

It was too late to try and be quiet. Snapping out of his shock, Charlie launched himself towards a metal box by the caretaker's desk that had a blinking red light. Ignoring the lock, he used the blood-covered claw of the hammer to prise open the box.

"Fletch, they're coming," Nora warned.

Fletcher tore his eyes away from Charlie and faced the corridor. Shadowy figures lumbered clumsily towards them. Nora sprung into action beside him, aiming a powerful kick at the nearest Zed and pushing it back into its fellows.

A Zed snuck up behind Fletcher, who felt its hot breath on the back of his neck. Holding the javelin horizontal with both hands, he pushed against the Zed's ribcage. He was rewarded with the snap of brittle bones as it was forced backwards. Instinctively, Fletcher stabbed with his javelin, the Zed impaling itself with its own momentum. He wrenched it free and aimed at the next attacker.

Fletcher risked a glance over his shoulder into the caretaker's office. Charlie was twisting dials and flicking switches, his hands fumbling.

Nothing.

"Any time today!" Nora cried out as she swung her baseball bat at the nearest snarling Zed.

"I'm trying!" Charlie called. Panic quivered in his voice.

Fletcher felt Nora grab his arm in the gloom. They were struggling against the swarm of Zeds they'd attracted. She pressed her back against his so that they fought opposing sides of the onslaught. Fletcher stabbed away blindly in the darkness with his javelin. He didn't know where he was aiming or which body parts he'd managed to spear. He just knew that with each jab he was keeping them at bay.

Fletcher felt his heart jump with relief as the lights flickered above their heads.

But he almost wished that he couldn't see the carnage they'd inflicted.

And the Zeds kept coming. Now, Fletcher could see just how many of them they'd stumbled across. The smell of rot overwhelmed him, and the Zeds snarled under the harsh lighting, their eyes bulbous and hungry.

"Run!" Charlie screamed.

Fletcher didn't need telling twice. He hurtled down the corridor, feet slipping on the gore ridden floor. He ducked under outstretched arms, ignoring the snapping teeth that threatened to tear the flesh from his body. Panting, he forced his way through the gap in the double doors, turning to hold them open as wide as the cables would allow. Nora ducked through next, her face streaked with blood and sweat. Then Charlie slipped through, just in time to stop one of the Zeds grabbing him.

Nora and Fletcher pressed their weight against the wooden doors with all their might. Charlie desperately threaded and wound the cables through the handles, pulling them taut. The three of them stood back, watching the doors struggle against the weight of the Zeds on the other side. The doors strained and retracted like lungs breathing in and out.

"We are never," Nora gasped, "*ever* doing that again."

"...and then I slid on my stomach between the legs of one Zed," Fletcher said animatedly, recounting a rather embroidered version of the events in the basement to Patrick. Patrick was listening with rapt attention, humoring Fletcher kindly. He sipped his mug of tea, catching Zoe's eye and smiling.

"Calm down, Indiana Jones," Nora said. She rolled her eyes. "The closest you came to a stunt was when you tripped up the stairs in the cafeteria."

Fletcher scowled at Nora. This was *his* moment and he was proud of what they'd achieved in the basement. It wasn't Patrick or Zoe who had fought off the Zeds; it had been him, the youngest and smallest of their bunch. He had felt his chest swell with pride when he'd returned triumphantly to the cafeteria with Charlie and Nora. They'd been greeted by the cheers and smiles of the younger students, holding their heads high as heroes.

"Stunts or no stunts, you did a really good job down there," Patrick assured Fletcher.

"We're grateful - to all of you," Zoe added. The corners of her brown eyes creased as she beamed at them. "It feels like a win, doesn't it? When all we've done so far is lose."

"I did think we were done for," Charlie admitted, running a hand over his short hair and allowing a nervous smile. "When that Zed attacked me in the office...I'm surprised you didn't hear the racket we caused."

"So much for stealth," Nora joked. She drummed her acrylic nails on the table. It was a habit that Fletcher had noticed before, and he wondered whether she was anxious. She maintained a tough exterior, but Fletcher knew she'd been scared in the basement. They all were. How could they not be, when they were fighting for their lives in the dark, unable to discern where the next attack would come from?

"Well, at least we've saved the frozen hash browns," Nora added dryly. "I wonder what our next mission will be?"

"We really need to get you some coffee, huh?" Charlie said. He nudged her. "You're getting cranky."

Nora sighed and rolled her eyes. "I'm going stir crazy in this school. Great, we managed to get the power back on. Woo hoo. But I just feel like we're sitting ducks here." She gazed longingly towards the windows, where the inky darkness of the night sky twinkled. "I'm desperate to see what's going on out there. We've waited long enough to be rescued. This isn't a life for us."

The group fell silent, each pondering their own thoughts. Deep down, Fletcher knew that Nora was right. They'd stayed at the school because they thought it was their safest option. And maybe it was, for a while. But the Zeds were breaking through the barricades each day, and Fletcher knew their group wasn't strong enough to defend themselves as it was, let alone if more Zeds came from outside the school. There had to be a better option.

And as much as Fletcher liked his new companions, he knew that somewhere out there, his real family might be waiting for him. If they were still alive, if there was still a chance to find them, he had to track them down.

"We can't go out there now," Charlie said gently to Nora. "I know you like taking risks, but you haven't got a death wish."

"I know *that*," Nora mumbled, examining her nails. "I just hate wasting time. What if there are other survivors out there? People who can help us? I can't ride out the apocalypse babysitting this lot."

Fletcher felt himself blush, which Nora quickly noted.

34

"Not you, Fletch," she added. "You're one of us. You don't mind getting your hands dirty."

"Or sliding around killing Zeds," Patrick added, winking at him. Fletcher allowed himself a small smile.

"I agree that it's too dangerous to assume we're safe here," Charlie said. "The generators we just switched on aren't a mains power supply; they will run out eventually. I'd rather we scope out an escape plan whilst we've got supplies, rather than leave it until we're desperate."

"I'm happy to come with you," Fletcher said immediately. Maybe it was the adrenaline still coursing through his veins, but he felt somehow invincible. He'd fought off the Zeds, and he'd made it out *alive*. He was untouchable.

"You've been through a lot tonight," Zoe said gently. "Get some rest. Tomorrow, you guys can scope things out. See what it's like before we decide to leave, like we agreed. I can hold down the fort here whilst you're gone. Maybe start getting things prepared for if we have to go anywhere…"

As Patrick and Zoe took up watch over the opposite sets of double doors, Fletcher curled up under a blanket on one of the spongy gym mats. He could already hear Charlie snoring from the mat he shared with Nora. Charlie slept with a baseball bat in one hand over their blanket, ready for anything the night may throw at them. Fletcher himself kept his hand clasped around the handle of the knife he'd taken from the kitchen. Even in sleep, they couldn't truly trust being safe.

Restless, Fletcher turned on his back and faced the ceiling. It was only his second night in the school - that he was conscious for, anyway - but he felt that he already understood the claustrophobia that Nora spoke of. Down in the basement, it had been dangerous, but that was the most alive Fletcher had felt since waking up. He didn't *enjoy* fighting the Zeds, but he also didn't enjoy sitting around in the cafeteria all day waiting - though what they were waiting for, he didn't really know.

He guessed tomorrow, they would find out.

Chapter Four

Rori was getting used to being able to feel his heart in his throat. As he swung his empty backpack over his shoulder and headed out to the car, he questioned whether he should be going on the scouting trip after all. He felt unreliable, like he would freak out at the worst possible moment and get everyone else in trouble.

The other volunteers didn't seem quite as on edge as he was. Heidi and Eliza were arguing by the car over something trivial that only siblings would argue about. Cassie was saying a quiet goodbye to Poppy a short distance away, their voices hushed. The calmest of them all was Luke, who was already sitting in the driver's seat, his face solemn as he ignored everyone else around him.

Rori questioned what he was even bringing to the team. Luke was ruthless, and the only one able to drive. Heidi was able to tap into a frenzy around the rotters, barely thinking as she slashed them down. Cassie and Eliza were a little more calculated, falling in formation with one another as they took on the hordes.

But Rori recalled how he felt when he was back at the college, battling his way through the rotters. He remembered how the terror consumed him to the point where he felt like he was on autopilot, only surviving it all because his body told him he had to. If it was left to his own decision making, he was sure he would have died on the first day.

And now, he was heading back out there. Into the unknown. He'd laughed it off before. Humor had always been his best defense mechanism. But now that the time had come to actually leave the farm, he felt sick to his stomach. How could he put himself through all of that again by choice?

"Come on, Rori. It's rotter o'clock, let's get a move on," Heidi called over to him. He automatically grinned back at her, despite the nausea settling in his stomach. He wondered if maybe Heidi felt the same way he did. Maybe she was consumed with fear too, she just did a better job of hiding it.

Ginge and Warren stood in the front doorway, ready to see them off on their travels. It was starting to feel much more real, now. Cassie and Poppy returned from their goodbye chat, Poppy glancing reluctantly at Cassie as she retreated to the safety of the house. She clearly had no desire to watch the others drive away. Rori wondered if it was too late for him to back out too…

"You sure you won't come with us, Ginge?" Cassie asked her. She pressed the tip of the knife against her palm to check that it was sharp. "If things get ugly out there, we'll be down our best fighter…"

This was another reason that Rori was hesitant. There was no denying that Ginge was the strongest among them. Her years working on the farm had made her physically strong, and she wasn't afraid to get her hands dirty in a fight. She embodied all of the best parts of the others; their physical strength, their brains, their ruthlessness.The fact that she wouldn't be with them made Rori feel more than a little anxious.

"Someone has to protect the farm," Ginge pointed out. "I can't leave Cara here on her own with the kids…she's terrified enough as it is. Besides, I don't want to be away from them. In case something happens…"

And there it was. The unspoken thing playing on everyone's mind. They had no idea what was waiting for them out there. They might not make it back again. They could be dead by the end of the day. Rori's stomach churned uncomfortably at the thought. Somehow, it didn't even bother him so much, the idea of him dying. It was more the thought of watching everyone around him succumb to the rotters. The thought of them all screaming in pain as the rotters dug their teeth and nails deep into their skin…

Rori was sure he was going to be sick, but he said nothing as the others said their goodbyes. He wanted to help. He had no desire to become a burden to the group, and that meant getting stuck in, even when it was the last thing he wanted to do. He took a deep breath and told himself to grow up. This was life now. He only had two options: to survive, or to die.

He knew which option he preferred.

"Stay safe!" Ginge called out to them as they all piled into the car. The car had once been her mother's, but she had offered it up for the trip. Luke had pointed out that it would be less conspicuous and easier to navigate than the bus they'd arrived in.

With Luke in the driver's seat, Rori piled in the back with Heidi and Eliza. Cassie took her position in the passenger seat up front, unfolding a map on her lap.

"I miss GPS," Cassie muttered as she scanned the crumpled piece of paper in front of her. Rori kept his head down and said nothing, swallowing down his nerves until he felt a sharp, bony elbow digging into his ribs.

"Hey," Heidi said, frowning at him. "You alright?"

Rori swallowed. "Yeah just, um, car sick."

Heidi cocked an eyebrow suspiciously. "We're not even moving yet."

"And yet I'm already sick of the car."

"I second that," Luke said. "I still think this a terrible idea."

"Well, the sooner we get it over and done with, the sooner you can complain about the trip from the safety of Ginge's house," Heidi said. She patted the back of Luke's headrest. "Giddy-up."

Rori managed the smallest of smiles. Their situation wasn't ideal. He was still scared of what was to come. But in such a short amount of time, he had come to care for and trust the people he was going through the whole ordeal with. He knew that if he had to be out there, in the unknown, he was safest with those four people in the car.

"Alright, everyone shut up. If we're doing this, we're doing it my way, and I don't want any of Heidi's mindless chatter while I navigate the roads," Luke said. Heidi opened her mouth to retort, but Luke turned and gave her such a glare that she immediately sank back in her seat. She pulled a face that seemed to say *what's with this guy?* Rori smirked as Luke began the drive to the garden center.

It wasn't far to drive, according to Cassie's calculations from the map, but Luke took the roads so slowly that it would likely take them twice as long to get there. They trundled along at a snail's pace, all of them keeping a watchful eye on their surroundings. The road was straight and long with open land all around them, so they could see any movement a mile off. Still, even though the fields were quiet, Rori's heart hammered against his chest. He had visions of a whole horde of rotters appearing suddenly from within the trees, their hands outreached toward them, their mouths gaping hungrily. Rori shuddered and tried to rid himself of the thought. He couldn't let his anxiety consume him. Not now.

"Next left," Cassie told Luke quietly. They were close to the nearest town, now, and Rori knew that was where the landscape was likely to change for them. Out at Ginge's farm, they didn't have to worry about neighbors turning and coming their way. He guessed that's why they'd been spared much action so far.

But the town would be another story. The area was more built up. It was likely to be crawling with rotters. Maybe even faces they recognised. He felt Heidi stiffen a little beside him, her hand turning over her screwdriver on her lap. He wanted to reach for her hand, to calm her, but he didn't have anything comforting to offer. She was right to be nervous, just as he was. It was better that they didn't let their guard down.

The car was silent save for the creaking of the changing gears and the hum of the engine. Luke indicated out of habit, even though there wasn't a single other car in sight. And then he turned into the road that would take them to the town center.

And all of a sudden, it felt like the car was too loud, like they were attracting too much attention. Rori wondered whether people were locked up inside the houses they passed, surviving, tensing at the sound of any noise they heard outside.

He began noticing little details of the homes they passed. Things that made them different to how they would have been a week before. Bloodstains on doorsteps. Boarded windows that once let light shine through. Shifting curtains in upstairs rooms, where people were making their stand, looking out for danger. Rori couldn't decide whether he was relieved that people were still alive and fighting, or anxious about what their survival instincts might push them to do.

And then there was the chaos in the town center. They sighted their first rotters, milling around sluggishly and without purpose. They seemed to be converging around the corner stores and the local supermarket, the places where people would have been gathered when it all happened. It was clear that there had been some kind of massacre there, judging by the blood stained pavements, smashed windows, abandoned cars. There was no telling whether anyone at all had gotten out alive.

At the sound of the car engine, the rotters began to amble toward them, their heads cocked to the side in interest. They were slow, but persistent. It seemed like they'd be willing to follow them wherever they went. Rori didn't miss the moment when Luke put his foot down on the accelerator and sped them away.

It was a relief when they carried on through the residential areas instead. The solemn quiet was better than seeing the masses of rotters, even if it was unclear if human life remained there at all.

"We're not far now," Cassie murmured, her voice low as though the rotters might hear them talking and pounce out of nowhere. "We should be about to reach the main road, so take a right turn and then it's just straight on."

Luke nodded silently. Rori could see that his knuckles were white on the steering wheel. The car felt uncomfortably hot, all of them breathing in the same stale air, but none of them dared to crack a window. It felt like an invitation for the rotters to get inside.

"Not long now," Luke murmured, but Rori thought he was talking to himself more than anyone else. He turned the car onto the main road.

And then he immediately slammed on the brakes.

Rori's heart leapt into his throat. The entire road was crowded with rotters. Dozens of them. They were acting as a very effective roadblock, crowding close together and bumping into one another.

"What are they all doing there?" Luke whispered, trying to peer closer. Rori craned his neck, and then wished that he hadn't.

In the middle of the roadblock, there was a convoy of three cars, probably filled with people who had the same idea as them. But the cars were overrun now, and Rori was sure that whoever had been inside those cars was either dead or about to be. There was no way anyone could make a dash from the car to get away. Not with such a thick crowd of rotters clumped around them.

"Turn around," Rori said urgently. "We have to go."

"No shit," Luke murmured, fighting with the gear stick to put them in reverse. The engine complained loudly at his jittery movements, causing some of the rotters to turn their attention toward them. The car jerked and then the engine died.

"Fuck," Luke growled, restarting the car. As it came to life, he was more restrained in his actions, trying to slowly ease the car into the right direction. Rori's heart was pummeling hard as the rotters changed their course toward their car. One was close enough that Rori could see the drool hanging from its decaying lips, hear the guttural moans forcing themselves out of its body. It reached out a hand and slapped it against the window on Eliza's side, making her jerk in horror.

"Luke…"

"I know, I know," Luke snapped, finally veering the car to the left and getting some speed behind them. Rori was sweating now, not daring to look back behind them and see whether they were being pursued. Surely they must be?

"Well, the thrills just keep coming," Heidi murmured, sinking low in her seat as though to hide from the oncoming horde. "What now? That was the best route to the garden center."

"We should go back," Luke said firmly. "We're low on petrol, and there's a fucking huge group of rotters just behind us. We were pushing it making this trip, petrol wise, and I don't want to take a risk that isn't worth it. I'd rather take a loss and keep my limbs."

"Wait, so that's it? We're giving up?" Heidi argued. "If we go back with nothing, then we're right back to square one. We'll have to venture out again at some point, and things might get worse out here. We're not even going to try?"

"Didn't you hear me? We're low on petrol."

"So we'll get some more. It might even be our last opportunity. And if we need to make any more detours, we don't want to end up with a dead car. Then we'd really be in deep trouble."

"I think she's got a point," Cassie murmured. "Especially about the petrol. If we can find a gas station, we might be able to fill up the tank, maybe grab some supplies from the store. Then, if we feel okay about it, we can plan a new route to the garden center."

Rori bit the inside of his cheek. It was a logical plan, and yet it filled him with dread. It wasn't what they'd agreed on when they left the house. If things had already gone wrong, what else might turn their trip sour?

"I guess we'll take it to a vote. I vote no," Luke said. He swiveled around to look at Rori. "What about you? You've got some sense."

Rori smiled at him. "Stop flirting with me, you."

"Don't flatter yourself. Are you in or not?"

"I don't know…you're not giving me much time to think about it."

Luke sighed, turning his attention back to the road. "Eliza?"

Eliza had been very quiet since they'd got in the car. She looked especially pale now after their encounter with the rotters. She swallowed. "I think it depends how long we think we're going to have to hold out. Seems to me like we're going to need to survive on our own for a while. And in theory, it's better to take risks now than a week or two down the line. That's when people will be more desperate. I think if we're doing this…it has to be today." She paused. "But that doesn't mean I *want* to do it."

"We can't go back now," Heidi insisted. "I like Cassie's plan. I say we go for it."

Rori hesitated for a moment, glancing at Heidi. Her eyes were hopeful as she returned his gaze. He swallowed. "Okay. I'm in."

Heidi nodded solemnly, her way of thanking him. He sighed. At the end of the day, he was always going to back Heidi. Eliza was nodding too.

"I swear you guys have a death wish," Luke muttered, realizing he was outnumbered. "Let's see if we can find a gas station, then."

Ginge climbed carefully up the ladder to the attic. It had served as a safe place for them all to sleep when any of them were actually able to close their eyes and get some rest. But above all, it had become the place where Cara and the kids spent almost all of their time.

As Ginge's head popped into the attic, she saw Cara sitting on a mattress, her eyes red and raw from crying. Billy and Hannah were distracted by a jigsaw, ignoring their sister. She did little but cry anymore. Ginge tried not to sigh as she hauled herself up into the attic room and approached her sister.

Cara sniffled, avoiding Ginge's gaze. They sat side by side for a while in silence, watching the kids playing. But Ginge knew she had to coax her sister out of her shell at some point. She couldn't stay up in the attic forever.

"You know, Poppy could use a hand with some of the chores, if you're up for it?"

Cara shook her head. "I don't…I don't want to go down there."

Ginge's first reaction was to be irritated. The rest of them were making their situation work, so why couldn't she? But she took one look at her sister and knew that she was never made for this kind of a life. She was too young to be prepared for such change and too old to be hiding out with the little kids.

The truth was, Ginge needed her to step up. They were stretched thin enough as it was. She wasn't asking for much. Maybe some help with washing out clothes, or scrubbing dishes, or making dinner. She wasn't asking her to go out there and kill the rotters herself. And yet Cara still made her feel like she was asking for far too much.

"Cara, you know you can't stay up here forever, right?"

Cara hugged her knees, sniffing. "Well, why not? There's nothing out there worth leaving this room for. I'm safe up here."

Ginge chewed her lip. "I know. But this isn't *life* up here. The rest of us are making the best of this. Or trying to, at least. We have to keep going."

"What for?"

Ginge opened her mouth to speak, but nothing came out of her mouth. Because Cara was right. There wasn't much that seemed worth living for. It would be so much easier to just hide away and wait for better days…

Ginge sucked in air and tried to think of good things. As she closed her eyes, the first thing that came to her mind was Warren. Sweet, mild-mannered Warren. The city boy making a life out in the country. He followed her around like a lost puppy, a little clumsy and eager to please, but she didn't mind in the slightest. In fact, she enjoyed the company.

And then there were all the other things she'd managed to cling on to for the past week. Her home. Her friends. The fact that she

45

was alive. She glanced at Cara and willed her to see the world through her eyes. Life had given them lemons, but she planned to make lemonade until the juices ran dry.

"Bad days always pass," Ginge told Cara softly. "I know it feels impossible to think that at the moment. I know you miss Mum and Dad. I miss them too. But we have each other. There may still be a way out of this whole thing. And then when this is over, we can go back to the life we had before."

Cara's lip wobbled, but she nodded slowly. Ginge placed a hand on her sister's shoulder gently. Sometimes she didn't understand her sister at all. Sometimes, she felt like she was from a different planet. But at other times, she saw someone who made perfect sense to her. Someone who she wished she could be. Because sometimes, Ginge wanted to be the one who got to curl up and cry. She wished she had been born second, or third, or fourth. Life would be easier that way.

But life would never be easy again. That's why Ginge needed Cara to step up too. If Ginge didn't make it, it would be Cara's job to keep the family alive. She had to know that she could count on her.

"Let's leave the kids up here for a while. They'll be alright on their own. Hannah will keep an eye on Billy, won't you?"

Hannah nodded without even looking up from her puzzle, her tongue sticking out from the corner of her mouth. Ginge pulled Cara to her feet and guided her over to the ladder. She could feel her sister's hand trembling.

"I can't, I can't," Cara whispered, staring down the ladder to the house below. Ginge gripped her sister's hand harder.

"You can," she said sternly. "And you're going to."

Cara sniffled, looking down below her anxiously. Then, slowly, she let go of Ginge's hand and began to clamber down the ladder. Ginge watched her sister in pride. It wasn't much, but it was a start. She'd faced her fear and that's all she could ask of her.

Ginge followed her down the ladder and watched as Cara headed for the kitchen in search of Poppy. She let out a quiet sigh. Her job as big sister was done, at least for a while.

"You're good with her."

Ginge turned around to see Warren standing at the base of the ladder. His hair was damp from the shower and he was smiling softly at her. She shrugged.

"I guess someone has to be. I'm the only family she has left to look up to. I have to take charge."

Warren nodded. "I know. I just meant…well, I don't think I could do it. You always have to be the brave one…that takes a lot."

Ginge felt a lump in her throat. He was right. She knew she had a hard exterior. She knew that people always saw her as the confident, cool-headed one. No one ever worried after her the same way because she was capable of looking after herself. But that didn't mean that she didn't want to give in, sometimes, and have someone hold her for a change.

She turned her back on Warren, not wanting him to see the tears gathering in her eyes. But then he did something that sent a shockwave through her body. His hand brushed over her shoulder, making her skin tingle. It only lasted for a moment, but she felt his hand on her long after he moved away, like a tattoo on her skin.

"You don't always have to be so strong around me," Warren said gently. And then he was gone, leaving Ginge with the lasting feeling that maybe she did have weaknesses after all.

"There. Up ahead."

Eliza peered through the window to see what Cassie was pointing to. There was a seemingly empty gas station up ahead. Somehow, the fact that it was quiet made Eliza feel more nervous than relieved.

"Alright. We get in and out as quickly as possible. Deal?" Luke asked.

"No arguments from me," Rori murmured. Eliza chewed her lip. "So we're really going to steal?"

Heidi stared at her sister. "Now is not the time to get a moral compass, Eliza. It's a gas station. It's not a local business or something. We're talking about taking some petrol and some snacks so that we don't die. I don't call that stealing."

"I know that…but what if we get in trouble?"

"You weren't so concerned about breaking the law the other day when you went on a murder spree of the rotters," Luke pointed out dryly. Eliza stared at him in horror and he shrugged. "Rotters used to be people. It counts."

"That was a matter of life and death."

Heidi spoke up before Luke could chip in. "Who's going to stop us? I'm pretty sure everyone else has bigger problems on their hands than us nabbing a few snacks from an abandoned shop. Hell, I bet somebody already ransacked the place. If we're not quick, there may only be prawn cocktail crisps left…"

Eliza didn't like the idea of them stealing, all the same. A week ago, she wouldn't have done it, so why should she do it now? She knew that logically, that was ridiculous. The rules were different now, and she had to get used to them. But still, something about their little mission felt very off.

Luke pulled the car up next to one of the gas pumps and got out so quickly that he'd barely killed the engine before he exited the vehicle. Eliza watched as the others piled out of the car. She hesitated for a moment before she grabbed her knife.

She felt as though she might need it.

"Keep your eyes peeled," Luke said to Rori. "I don't want to be ambushed by rotters while we're filling up. Cassie, Eliza, Heidi…if you're going inside, you should do it now. I want to be out of here in five minutes."

Heidi took the empty rucksack from Rori and headed straight for the small convenience store attached to the gas station. Cassie followed her, her own knife at the ready. Eliza had no idea what they were about to find inside. From the outside, it looked relatively untouched by the chaos of the past week. Did that mean it really was a goldmine for them? Had passersby overlooked it when searching for supplies? Or were people just not that desperate yet? Their group was bigger than most, and that meant more mouths to feed. Maybe they were striking before everyone else because they needed to most.

Eliza told herself that what they were doing was necessary as they walked cautiously toward the store. Cassie took the lead, pushing gently on the door, which opened with ease accompanied by a tinkling bell. As they stepped inside, Eliza had the very distinct feeling that they should turn back.

But they didn't.

Inside was like a treasure trove. The shelves still seemed to be fully stocked, filled with endless packaged food, magazines and toiletries. Behind the counter, there was a glass cabinet that still contained a wide range of alcohol and cigarettes. The entire place looked as though it was frozen in time, untouched by the horrors that the rest of the town had endured.

And for some reason, that made Eliza anxious.

"Bloody hell, there's enough in here to feed a small army," Heidi exclaimed. She shoved a few things into her rucksack, seeming more interested in the chocolate bars and crisps on offer than the cans of soup and tinned fruit. Eliza rolled her eyes and carefully picked up a can of peaches. It felt wrong even holding it in her hand, knowing that she planned to take it away without paying for it. But the store was visibly empty. The place had clearly been untouched by the rotters. Heidi was right. If they didn't take it, someone else would eventually. And after a week of worrying about food and where it would come from next, the thought of having enough for everyone to last a while seemed worth the discomfort that settled in Eliza's stomach.

The three of them worked quickly, filling their bags with as much as they could carry. Eliza's caution was thrown to the wind as she swept an entire shelf of tins into her bag, causing the bag to dip immediately. They were making quite a lot of noise, but Eliza hadn't seen any rotters since the blockade, and she knew they'd be out of there soon enough -

"Stop what you're doing."

Eliza's head snapped up. Two people, a young man and an older woman, had emerged from hiding. She could see now that the storeroom door was open and they were waiting in the doorway. She guessed they'd been holed up there for some time.

"We don't mean to bother you," Cassie said, taking a step back even though the two strangers were on the other side of the store. "We just came to get some food for us and our friends..."

"And what makes you think you're entitled to any of this stuff?" the young man growled, stepping a little closer. The man was wearing a burgundy shirt with a nametag on the pocket, like he'd just come straight from work. He seemed like just an ordinary guy, but Eliza's heart jolted when she saw that he held a knife in his hand. Cassie put her hands in the air defensively.

"I'm sorry, we-"

"I worked here," the man snarled, advancing further toward the three girls, who instinctively clumped together. "If anyone should have this stuff, it's me."

"Please. We didn't mean any harm," Cassie said, her voice wavering. "The door was open, we-"

"I suggest you leave and don't bother coming back," the man said, his knife steady in his hands. It was almost as though he'd done this before. "Because if I see your faces here again, I might not be so kind."

Heidi grabbed Cassie by the arm and pulled her back toward the door, the fear in her eyes clear as day. Eliza didn't often see her sister looking scared, but when she did, she knew it was time to run. They backed out of the shop, stumbling over one another as they hurried to get back to the car.

"Time to go," Heidi hissed urgently at Luke and Rori, who didn't seem to have realized how things had gone south inside. But they didn't hesitate for a moment as they loaded back into the car. Luke's foot was on the gas before they'd even fully shut the car doors.

There was the collective sound of them all catching their breath.

"What happened in there?" Rori breathed. "Rotters?"

"No," Eliza whispered. "Humans."

Chapter Five

Fletcher woke to crisp autumn sunlight streaming into the cafeteria. He sat up groggily, wiping sleep from his eyes.

"I thought you were going to wake me for a watch," he said accusingly to Zoe.

"Well, good morning to you too!" Zoe answered brightly. "I was, but you looked so peaceful…."

Fletcher had a sneaking suspicion that Zoe was trying to force him to rest. And after the events of the previous night, he could hardly complain. He had to admit to himself that his body ached from the physical exertion of the fight, especially after being out of action for a week. It was like his body was telling him to take it easy, but that wasn't exactly going to be an option. Not when there was so much to do.

He looked around at the rest of the students waking up, watching Patrick dish out mugs of tea and cartons of juice.

"Come on, look alive!" Charlie said. A groan surfaced from a lumpy shape that lay curled beneath a blanket on the mat he shared with Nora.

Charlie placed a mug of coffee where Fletcher assumed Nora's head was. The shape moved reluctantly under the blanket.

"Has anyone told you how truly *insufferable* you are in the morning," Nora grumbled, glaring at Charlie from under her dark curls as she sat up.

"You, every morning," Charlie joked. He planted a quick kiss on her forehead that Nora completely ignored. Fletcher felt his lips twitch into a smile. In a matter of days, he'd grown rather fond of their mismatched group. A niggling feeling in his stomach told him to remember this morning, this feeling. To remember Nora shoving Charlie away from her steaming mug of coffee, and the way Zoe laid her cheek affectionately against Patrick's hand on her shoulder. Things were good. Or as good as they could be.

When Nora was finally eased from her cocoon of blankets, she, Charlie and Fletcher readied themselves for their excursion. They gathered their weapons as Zoe forced an individually wrapped breakfast pastry on each of them along with bottled water. They hovered by the door, waiting for Patrick. Charlie was quietly calm and Nora seemed nonchalant as she examined her nails. Fletcher bounced on the balls of his feet with nervous energy. He just wanted to get out there, to get it over and done with.

Patrick joined them a moment later, pulling a hoodie over his nurses' scrubs.

"I'm ready to go," he said. He glanced back at Zoe guiltily, where she hung back from them by the door. He lowered his voice to Fletcher. "She wants me to stay, but I need to see this for myself. I need to know what we're up against."

"I know the feeling," Fletcher mumbled.

Zoe squeezed Patrick's hand one last time as she ushered them out of the cafeteria.

"Good luck," she whispered to them all, before shutting the door behind them and leaving them alone.

Patrick and Fletcher fell into step behind Charlie and Nora. They set off down the corridor, where Nora and Charlie quickly dealt with several Zeds that crossed their path. To them, it almost seemed like second nature, now.

They emerged from the school into bright daylight, and Fletcher felt himself gulp in the fresh air greedily. He didn't realize how stale the air in the school had become until now. Stepping out of the school, he could almost convince himself that he'd been let out of class early.

That was, until he spotted the corpses.

Flies buzzed around the decaying bodies. The stench of death wafted over them, carried by a gentle breeze, and Fletcher covered his nose instinctively. Patrick laid a hand on Fletcher's elbow, guiding him forward.

"Don't look," Patrick whispered. "There's nothing we can do for them now."

Out past the school gates, the four walked quietly down the main road that led from the school into the town center. Stepping off the pavement into the road, they weaved through abandoned cars. Zeds were trapped inside some of them, banging furiously on the windows with bloodied fists as they passed. Fletcher felt sick in his stomach when, through an open car door, he spotted an empty baby seat in the back.

Curtains twitched in the windows of houses that overlooked the main roads. Whether the cause was living residents or Zeds, Fletcher didn't know. Dismembered bodies of Zeds littered one neat front garden that they passed and Fletcher looked away quickly. There was something deeply unsettling about seeing a bloodied hand next to a children's swing set.

They reached the cobbled town center in no time, their journey silent save for the occasional "watch out" or "over there" whispered between them as a rogue Zed approached. They wandered past the fast food stores, the cinema and the pharmacy to the town square. The clock tower marked the center of the square, opposite the town hall where many of their parents had been photographed on their wedding days.

It was eerily quiet. So quiet that even the sound of their footsteps sounded too loud, like it was going to attract an entire horde of Zeds.

"You think it's abandoned?" Fletcher whispered. Charlie shook his head slowly.

"I don't think so. I think something must have happened here…maybe it drew the Zeds out of the town center. I'm sure they'll be back."

Fletcher jumped as the clock tower chimed, sending the murder of crows that were fighting over scraps of bread skyward. His eyes darted nervously around the square, but all was still. All was calm.

HAVEN, proclaimed large lettering on a white sign that was propped outside the town hall. Charlie and Nora looked from the sign back at the two boys, and shrugged. "It's worth a shot," Nora suggested. "That's what we came here for."

Their hopes were dashed moments later. Pushing into the town hall, they found it abandoned and in complete disarray.

There were signs that survivors had indeed made a stand. A pile of squashy sleeping bags were tucked in a corner, along with a half-drank crate of plastic water bottles. There were cans of soup and other dried foods packed in a bin, as if ready for transportation. There were batteries, torches and first-aid kits; useful things that Fletcher slipped into the rucksack that Zoe had given him.

Fletcher found himself wandering from room to room curiously. What had caused everyone to leave? How many survivors had made it to the "haven"? Where was the so-called haven now?

He turned a corner and stopped dead in his tracks.

"What are you looking at?" Patrick asked, popping his head around a door.

"The messages," Fletcher said sadly. The wall was covered with ripped fragments of paper that overlapped one another, each with a handwritten note scrawled on. Some were practical messages - containing an address, or a meeting location - whereas others were more personal. *Daddy, please find us* was written in large letters by a messy hand, next to one that simply said, *Kate, I love you.*

Fletcher felt a lump rise in his throat. He felt like he was intruding on the most private, intimate moments of these strangers' lives. He could almost feel the urgency in the messages, the desperation and love that bled into the paper with the words. He wondered how many of the notes were written by people he knew; neighbors, classmates, the old lady who ran the corner shop on the way to school. His eyes scanned the notes curiously, until they found one note, and his heart leapt.

Cassie & Fletcher.

He recognised her handwriting immediately. His mum had always curled the "C" in his sister's name. Hands shaking, hardly daring to believe his luck, Fletcher carefully moved aside the note covering it - *Don't go home, it's not safe* - to gently tug the scrap of paper from the wall.

Cassie & Fletcher, we're waiti-

Fletcher held the fragment of paper delicately between his thumb and forefinger.

The message had been ripped.

"Mum," Fletcher whispered. "Dad."

Patrick hovered by his shoulder. "Is that from your parents?"

Fletcher ignored him. "Where is it?"

"What?"

"The rest of the note! I've got to find it!" Fletcher cried. Tears were streaming down his face now, as he fell to the floor and searched desperately through the debris and rubbish that lay there. His hands skimmed over crisp packets and empty drink cans that he sent rattling across the floor in his haste. "It has to be somewhere-"

"Fletcher," Patrick murmured. He squatted down next to the younger boy and put a hand on his shoulder.

"It's here, I know it - "

Patrick squeezed his shoulder gently. He let Fletcher search the fragments of curled paper that littered the floor, which were soon discarded. When he'd checked each one twice, Fletcher got back to his feet. His eyes darted anxiously over the wall of messages again. "Maybe someone pinned it back up…"

"Fletcher, it could be anywhere now," Patrick said quietly. "*They* could be anywhere now."

"They tried to find us - "

"I know."

Patrick opened his arms as Fletcher crumpled against him, sobbing. He patted the younger boy's back as Fletcher heaved. Fletcher knew that they were exposed, that he shouldn't be making himself so vulnerable when they were in unknown territory, but his emotions were getting the better of him.

His sobs died down a few minutes later. Patrick held him the whole time, his embrace a sanctuary when the rest of the world was in ruin. Fletcher gasped for air, trying his hardest to pull himself together. Patrick rubbed his back.

"I'm sorry, Fletcher…we have to go," Patrick told him. "It's time now. It's not safe here."

Fletcher nodded. His eyes were red, the surviving half of the note crumpled in a tight fist. He never wanted to let it go. The last scrap of hope that tied the four members of his family together.

Patrick guided him gently out of the building, never pushing him to hurry despite the urgency of the situation. Fletcher was grateful for his kindness, but it only made him miss his family more. His mother, the sweetest and kindest woman he'd ever known. His father, the jokester of the family, but always a shoulder to cry on too. And Cassie…Cassie…

His best friend. His sole confidant when times got hard. The person he trusted more than anyone on Earth…

Are you still looking for me, Cassie?

Fletcher felt drained as they headed outside. They found Charlie and Nora waiting for them outside the town hall.

"I told you there would be other survivors," Nora said triumphantly. She was holding a map proudly. Patrick and Fletcher stood behind her as she opened it up.

"There," she said. She pointed on the map, where there was a circle in black marker pen. "Someone left this map behind. They must have been planning to head here, where it's marked."

"That's the national park," Patrick said. "That's *miles* from here, Nora."

"I know that, but it's something," Nora insisted. "Okay, we might not get there, but we might find people on the way. It's something to aim for at least."

"Nora's right," Fletcher said. He could still feel the paper crumpled in his fist. It had given him hope, briefly, that he could find his family. Maybe some of the other kids would be luckier than he was. They deserved the chance, at least. And maybe his own family would be there, waiting for him.

He had to hope.

"We can't isolate ourselves in the school forever," Nora said. "It was safe, for a while, but it's not sustainable." She gestured to the map. "This is something to aim for. We can get a group together. Take the kids from the school, then build ourselves a mini army. You saw the movement in the houses on our walk down. They can't all be Zeds. Some of them have to be people too. Adults, perhaps. And if that's true…" She looked exhausted for a moment. "If that's true, then maybe we won't have to lead the way anymore."

"Then let's go tell them," Charlie said finally. "Let's not waste any more time."

Nora beamed at him. She folded the map and tucked it into the back pocket of her jeans. She and Charlie set off across the square, taking a shortcut through the alley behind a local fast food chain. Fletcher felt like dragging his feet, but he hurried to keep up with them. The quiet streets were putting him on edge, even more than before…

It happened in slow motion. They heard the guttural moan above their heads from a Zed trapped on the fire escape before it toppled over the railings above Charlie's head.

"Charlie!" Nora screeched. She launched herself towards him, pushing him to safety.

The Zed fell hard on top of Nora, sending her sprawling to the floor. It didn't falter for a moment, zoning in on the exposed flesh beneath her disheveled t-shirt.

For the rest of his life, Fletcher would never forget the cry that escaped Nora's lips as teeth sank into her shoulder.

Chapter Six

The farm group drove in silence for a while, still shell-shocked from their encounter at the gas station. Luke felt like he'd been holding his breath ever since they'd left the house, but he felt even more suffocated now. They'd been so busy worrying about what the rotters were capable of, they hadn't stopped to think about what other survivors might do to them.

Luke understood why the man at the gas station had been so territorial. They'd have acted exactly the same if it were Ginge's farm under siege. He was scared, just like the rest of them. He was protecting what little he had left in the world, even if it didn't technically belong to him. And things were different now. Personal possessions, money, clothes…all the things that seemed to matter before were no longer necessities. Their new currency was food, supplies, water. Anything that could keep them alive for just a little longer. And that meant that breaking into stores and taking whatever they fancied was no longer on the cards. They'd have to be smarter.

"This isn't the right route," Cassie said as Luke drove straight back toward Ginge's farm. "We're going further away from the garden center."

"That's because we're not going there," Luke said firmly. "Haven't we had enough close calls for one day?"

"But we didn't get what we came for," Heidi argued.

"You got away from the convenience store with some food. You're lucky you still have your head, too. Those guys could have killed you. Do you understand that?"

"He wouldn't *actually* have hurt us," Heidi said, but Luke could sense the doubt in her tone. "Just because he waved a knife to scare us off, it doesn't mean he would've had the balls to actually use it."

"Did you really want to test that theory? Shall I turn around and go back, see if he'll stab you to prove me right?" Luke snapped. Heidi rolled her eyes.

"Obviously it was horrible. Obviously none of us want to go through that again. But everyone is in the same boat. Are you telling me that if someone came to the farm and started rooting for supplies, you wouldn't act the same? We made a mistake. It's done now and we learned from it. The garden center could be different."

"Or it could be exactly the same, or worse. We've got what we need for now. Our tank is full. We need to get the car home and only use it again in emergencies."

"How about a compromise?" Cassie reasoned. "Maybe we don't go to the garden center today…maybe instead, we stop somewhere on our route back and look for some extra supplies. We'll be more careful this time, and better prepared. There are five of us, we should be able to handle anything that comes our way."

Luke huffed out air in frustration. He knew, logically, that Cassie was probably right. They might as well take opportunities while they were already out in the open. But all he wanted was to get everyone back to the house safely. They had more supplies than when they'd left the house. Why couldn't that be enough for them?

"I don't see why we can't just be satisfied with the progress we made today. We took a big leap and it almost got us in trouble, twice. In this case, third time lucky sounds like a bad omen."

"I never took you to be superstitious, Luke," Heidi said coolly. "And it's not like you to back away from a challenge. So why don't you just slow down the car and we can see if we can spot any opportunities to pick up some stuff?"

Luke gritted his teeth. He was tired of everyone arguing with him, talking back to him as though he was the crazy one. But he slowed down the car anyway. He knew that the others wouldn't shut up until they'd done what they wanted to do.

They'd shut up pretty sharpish if they got themselves killed.

They drove slowly through the streets. The further they got away from the town center, the quieter the roads seemed to be. They saw a few rotters, but nothing like the roadblock several miles back. Luke found that if they stuck to the residential areas more, then it almost seemed like everything was normal.

Except that all of the driveways were missing cars. Some front doors were left wide open, as though someone had left in a hurry. Luke slowed curiously and peered into one of the houses as they passed it. There was no sign of life within these homes. It was like everyone on the street had the good sense to pack up and go when they had the chance. Where they'd gone to, Luke had no idea. Perhaps there was someplace safe far away, somewhere unaffected by the strangeness of the past week.

Whatever had happened, it presented them with an opportunity.

"Is this what you were hoping for, then?" Luke asked, slowing the car almost to a halt. "Do you want to check it out?"

"I'd say so," Cassie said, her hand already reaching to open her passenger door. "Stay with the car, if you want. We won't be long."

"We may need a getaway driver," Heidi added.

Luke stayed put as the others piled out of the car and shut the doors as quietly as they could. But, as they approached the house with the open door, their various weapons at the ready, Luke felt himself getting irritated at the thought of being left behind. He was no coward, and they'd need him if things went south. If they were determined to do this, then the least he could do was back them up.

He stepped out of the car cautiously and locked it up, shoving the keys in the pocket of his hoodie before bringing up the rear of the group, hobbling slightly on his swollen ankle. He only hoped it wouldn't hinder him if they needed to make a run for it.

Rori waited for a moment in the doorway, listening out for the sounds of the house with his head cocked. He reached his hand out as though to knock on the door before disguising his movement by running his hand through his blonde hair. Heidi sniggered quietly, not having missed the gesture.

"Get moving," Luke hissed at them. He didn't want to spend any more time in the house than they needed to. Rori hesitated for just another moment before moving as quietly into the house as he could. Everyone was slowly raising their various weapons, preparing for anything that might come their way.

Dead or alive.

They all took the same path through the house, quietly observing their surroundings like the intruders they were, making an effort not to touch anything. On the floor of the living room, they found a young man lying dormant on the ground with a knitting needle plunged through his eye socket. Blood and white foam lingered on the dead man's mouth, and his one good eye was still bloodshot, a telltale sign of the killer infection. His hand was reaching out, as though clawing toward something.

Or someone.

The house looked as though perhaps it had belonged to an older person, with several black and white photographs hung on the walls and a collection of vintage looking furniture. Luke felt like a detective as he tried to figure out the story of what had happened in that house. Perhaps the young man had been caring for an older person when he turned and forced them to flee their home, leaving the door open in the process...

Not that any of that mattered. The fact was, the house seemed abandoned, and that was a good thing for them. Luke began to move a little quicker through the lower level of the house, determined to find the goods so that they could get out of there.

"Bingo," Rori whispered as they all moved into the kitchen. The kitchen showed no signs of being ransacked. Perhaps they were the only ones who, so far, had been bold enough to go rooting through other people's homes. Luke strode toward the fridge and swung it open. The electricity still seemed to be working fine for the moment, and some of the food in the fridge was still in date.

"Let's hurry up and fill our bags so we can get out," Luke murmured. For once, nobody argued with him. They all moved with a sense of urgency now, not wanting to repeat the events at the convenience store. Luke could feel the blood thrumming through his eardrums as he shoved as much as he could into his bag. He was barely paying attention to what was still edible, simply desperate to get back home.

"Rori, with me," Luke murmured as the group continued to empty the kitchen of its stock. "Let's see if we can find anything else of use in this place."

"Get some bloody loo roll," Heidi whispered. "Just because the world has gone to shit, doesn't mean we don't need loo roll…"

"Charming," Luke muttered, but the item shot straight to the top of his list.

He and Rori moved slowly toward the staircase, like animals stalking prey in the wild. *Better to be the predator than the prey,* Luke thought to himself.

Each stair seemed to creak beneath their feet. Luke held his breath, scared to make any noise at all. He peered into the room on the left hand side of the staircase. Sat upright in a hideously upholstered armchair was a bloodied corpse, flesh and muscle picked clean from the bones. Flies buzzed around the carcass with a manic energy, trying to scavenge what remained. The corpse surveyed them out of empty eye sockets, hollowed out like caves into the skull.

The corpse had been decaying for longer than the one downstairs, and the bloody mess only confirmed that something had feasted on him at some point. The man had evidently been old when he died, judging by what was left of him, and he had already led a life of some description. Perhaps he was enjoying his retirement when he was killed. But the man downstairs…his life was barely beginning. To have all of that ripped away…it made Luke's stomach twist to think about.

A retching sound behind him made Luke turn. He saw Rori bent over double, unable to take the sight of the wreck of the man's body. Luke patted him on the back, the closest to affection he would ever get.

"Sorry," Rori muttered as he stood back up, wiping his mouth. He was even paler than he had been earlier. "That's been coming for a while."

"It's alright. We've really seen some shit today," Luke said. "But keep moving if you can."

The pair of them headed into the bathroom together and began to scoop up as many items as they could carry. Luke found himself shoving shampoo and soap into the pockets of his jeans, toothpaste into his hoodie, and even a razor which he tucked under his belt. He felt ridiculous, but he knew that the more they took away from their trip, the longer it would be before they'd have to venture out again, and that was enough to keep him going.

His foraging frenzy was interrupted by a loud shriek downstairs. He and Rori exchanged a look before hurtling toward the sound of the noise, all attempts at remaining undetectable forgotten. They dropped the supplies at the base of the stairs in their hurry.

They entered the living room just in time to see a rotter stumbling toward Heidi. She was backing away with her screwdriver raised, but not looking where she was going. She crashed against the wooden coffee table and fell to the floor, the breath knocked completely out of her lungs.

The sound of gnashing teeth reached Luke's ears as he watched the scene unfold. The screwdriver had fallen out of Heidi's grasp, and she was grappling for something else to use. As Luke surged forward to help, she dislodged the knitting needle from the dead man's eye and plunged it into the rotter's face. It squelched through the rotten flesh between the rotter's eyes and it fell dormant, crumpling to the ground.

Breathless, Heidi scrambled to her feet as the rotter fell down. Luke could see that the sudden appearance of the rotter had caught Heidi off guard. It was like she'd forgotten to arrange her face into its usual calm smirk. Now, she seemed much more flustered.

She managed to compose herself, wiping the knitting needle on her jeans. Then she tutted to herself.

"Poppy's going to kill me for getting blood on my jeans. *Again,*" she said conversationally, as though the last ten seconds hadn't just happened. She turned the knitting needle over in her hand. "I'm keeping this thing," she muttered. She glanced up. "The door was open. Luke, did you shut it when you came in?"

Luke's heart slammed hard against his chest. "I…I thought I did."

"Either you didn't or someone else opened it again. I'll bet anything those dumb creatures can't use a doorknob," Heidi said, wiping sweat from her face. "Which means that we might not be alone in here."

Luke's heart almost stopped altogether. Had someone seen them enter the house and followed them in? And if so, why? He felt sick, whipping his head around to check he wasn't being creeped up on. His t-shirt was damp and sticking to his skin with sweat.

Eliza and Cassie rushed in at the same moment.

"What happened?" Eliza asked, her eyes darting around the room to examine the chaos that had ensued after the attack.

"A rotter got in," Rori said, glancing over his shoulder. "The front door is wide open."

"How the hell…"

They all turned at the sound of a creak in the hallway. Standing on the stairway was a figure. Luke's heart jolted. A rotter?

No…the young man on the stairwell didn't seem like he had turned. He was wide-eyed, holding a pistol in his shaking hands.

His eyes were a piercing blue, and there was a shock of red hair atop his head. He didn't look to be much older than them, especially with the child-like fear in his eyes.

Here we go again, Luke thought.

"I don't want to hurt you," the young man said. He had a thick Scottish accent, and it took Luke a moment to process what he'd said. "I just wanted to talk."

The group stared back at the young man, all of them seemingly frozen in place. But Luke, spurred on by anger, stepped to the front of the group, glaring the young man down.

"You opened the door. You let the rotter in. You could have gotten us killed!" Luke snarled. The young man shook his head fervently.

"I didn't mean to. I saw you guys come in here…I haven't seen another soul all week. I've been living across the street on my own, but the food's all gone and I can't keep living alone…please, you have to understand-"

"What I understand is that you're reckless and we could have wound up dead if we weren't so well prepared to fight," Luke snapped. "You should leave. Take your gun and get out of here. If you don't want any trouble then leave us be."

The young man was trembling. He looked at the pistol in his hand, as if remembering that he was armed. He lowered the gun, placing it on the floor and holding his hands up, palms facing the group.

"Please. Don't make me go back out there alone. You guys seem to have your shit together. Where are you headed to? Maybe…maybe you could take me there with you."

"What?" Luke demanded, outraged at the very thought. This stranger, the man who had almost cost them everything, wanted them to take pity on him? What the hell was he thinking?

The young man began to descend the stairs, his hands in the air as though in surrender. "I'm Joe. I'm nineteen…I'm training as a carpenter. I've been renting a room in the house across the street while I study, but the owner...he turned. He turned days ago and I've been on my own ever since. I don't know anybody in this town...I have nowhere to go. Please, if you have a heart...let me come with you."

"I just had to put a knitting needle through a dead person's face to save my own butt," Heidi said, folding her arms across her chest. "That's on you. Why would we take you anywhere with us when you're clearly a liability? And you haven't exactly given yourself the best introduction. You were pointing a bloody gun at us..."

"Finally, you're talking sense," Luke muttered, never taking his eyes off Joe. But he had to admit, as stupid as Joe's actions had been, he looked like someone who could be of use to them. He was well-built, clearly strong. If he learned to be a little more street smart, he could be an asset to the group...

But that was ridiculous, because there was no way they were taking Joe with them. He was a stranger. A stranger who didn't know how to use his brain. There were already too many flaws in the group that Luke was concerned would get them killed, but adding another guy to the equation? It didn't make sense.

"Look," Joe said gently. "I know I made a bad impression. I was scared shitless, and I'm sorry. I never would've shot at you. There aren't even any bullets in the gun. It was my grandfather's, it's an antique. I just figured it would keep me safe from people if things turned nasty, maybe scare them off. I panicked, I pointed it. Please...if I stay holed up on my own, I'll go mad. Or I'll get myself killed. Everyone needs someone, right? I'll do anything. Please, I'll do anything."

Luke felt uncomfortable seeing the desperation in Joe's eyes. He watched as Joe kicked the gun across the floor towards Luke.

"I'm willing to do anything," Joe said, his eyes pleading. "Anything at all. And I swear, I won't get you guys in trouble again. I really won't."

"Look, Joe, it's not personal…" Cassie started.

"It is," Luke muttered. He glanced at the gun on the floor, wondering whether he should pick it up or not. His mum had a strict "no guns" policy with toys when he was growing up, and Luke wasn't sure he was ready to feel the weight of a real gun in his hands.

"It's just that we have enough problems as it is. Heidi's right, you almost got us killed. How do we know you're not going to do that again?"

Joe took a shaky breath. "Because…because I don't want to see anyone else die."

The comment hung heavy in the air between them all. Luke stared him down, trying to figure out if he meant it or not. But there was no time to process it, because that was when he heard the growling outside.

Luke pushed his way to the front door and felt his stomach drop at what he saw. Outside, a group of rotters were making their way down the street. It was almost like they were traveling in a pack, each of them with one goal in mind.

Human flesh.

They weren't far from the house, and they could clearly sense the group, clumped together like one big enticing six-course meal. They began to change their course, ambling toward them.

"It's time to go," Luke said, snapping his head around to look at his friends. "Rotters are coming."

"Wait!" Joe cried out, but the five of them were already rushing out of the house toward the car, grabbing their supplies along the way. Luke opened the car and threw open the trunk to ditch the things he'd had time to grab.

Luke hesitated for a moment, glancing back at the house. Joe was standing frozen in the doorway, his eyes filled with fear. Luke knew he was processing the fact that he was about to be left alone with a bunch of rotters, unarmed, with no one else to back him up.

He let out a grunt of frustration and ran back to the house. He reached out to grab Joe's arm, tugging him toward the car without thinking too much about the consequences. If he left Joe, he would die. That he was sure of. And he didn't want that on his conscience.

Joe followed him blindly, clearly too scared to protest. Without thinking, Luke saw the open trunk of the car and shoved Joe inside.

"Stay down," Luke snapped and slammed it shut. Looking behind him, he could see the rotters advancing at frightening speed, urged on by the smell of fresh meat. He scrambled toward the driver's seat and got in, not bothering to put on his seatbelt before he drove off at top speed.

There were a few moments of silence between the five of them. Then, Rori cleared his throat.

"Luke?" he asked pleasantly. "Did you just kidnap that young man?"

Chapter Seven

The trunk of the car was dark and musty. Still, Joe didn't think it was ever intended to have passengers. He curled himself into a ball and tried not to wince every time the car took an unexpected turn, throwing him this way and that. He couldn't believe this was happening to him. One minute, he'd been completely alone. Now, he was being bundled off to somewhere unknown with a bunch of strangers...

What did they plan to do with him when they got to their destination? He had no idea. The five of them were so young, and yet they seemed hardened to the world. Especially the guy in the burgundy hoodie, his deep blue eyes so intense as he stared Joe down...

He didn't know what these kids were capable of. He should never have followed them into that house. But what choice did he have? He'd been alone all week, locked up in his bedroom with only a bulletless gun to defend himself. He'd dealt with his landlord in ways he didn't even want to think about, and that made him a survivor. But if there had been more than one, he would have died. He had been waiting every day for someone to come along so he could find his way out of his own mess.

And yet now, he was in an entirely new mess. The group he'd found seemed capable of anything. They were clearly strong survivors. They'd made it this far, and they were brave enough to be wandering the dead-ridden streets. And if they were willing to deal with the dead so ruthlessly...how would they deal with the living?

Joe felt as though he could barely breathe. The road was getting bumpier now, like the country roads leading out of the town. Was that where they were taking him? It felt like they were going to the middle of nowhere. Joe didn't think he'd even be able to find his way back home if they did happen to let him go. So what were his options? Did he have any that wouldn't involve him getting killed?

Joe could hear the group arguing in the car, though their voices were muffled. He was sure that he was the subject of their conversation. He wished that he could just show them that he wasn't a liability, that he could be useful to them. But he could hardly make his case when he was stowed away in the back of their car. It was definitely up there with one of the weirdest moments of his life.

And scariest.

The car began to slow and Joe held his breath. He didn't know what was about to happen, but he sensed they were nearing the end of their journey. Whatever it was, he just hoped he'd get out of it alive.

The car parked up and he heard the slamming of doors as the others got out. His stomach twisted with anxiety. He wished he had something to defend himself with. Even then, though, there were five of them and one of him. He didn't think it was a fight he would stand any chance to win.

The trunk of the car suddenly opened, blinding Joe with the late afternoon sunlight. He blinked several times and felt rough hands grab his t-shirt, pulling him up out of the car. He just about managed to find his feet, still dazzled by the brightness as he was pulled along with whoever had a hold of him. He realized quickly that it was the boy in the burgundy hoodie. Luke, they'd called him.

"You don't have to do this," Joe said urgently. "I'm sorry about before. You don't need to…you don't need to hurt me…"

"What?" Luke said. "I've just saved you from that horde of rotters. Do you really think that means I want you dead?"

"Well, you do give off serious serial killer vibes sometimes," one of the girls - Heidi, Joe thought he heard her called - said. She still

72

had a knitting needle in her hand, and she was examining it with something close to pride.

Joe took a second to take in where they were. They were standing outside a pleasant bungalow surrounded by acres of fields and bare land. He could hear the distant sound of cows mooing. They were on a farm, he realized with surprise. Admittedly, it was the last place he'd ever expect to be kidnapped to, but it was so isolated that no one would ever hear him scream...

"What the hell is going on?" a girl with hair like fire asked as Luke hauled Joe toward the house. She was standing in the doorway, her arms folded. She looked, to Joe, like somebody he wouldn't want to cross. "What are you doing?"

"This idiot almost got us killed," Luke snapped, glaring at Joe.

"So we saved his life," Rori said.

"A bunch of rotters showed up," Luke continued. "We couldn't just leave him there to die. But don't worry. He's not staying."

"Calm down," Eliza, the quietest one, said gently. "He made a mistake. It happens to the best of us."

"Mistakes aren't an option anymore," Luke reminded her. "We can't afford for him to drag us down." Luke let go of Joe finally, but Joe could still feel his fingers digging into his arm. "We saved your ass. We got you out of the danger zone. Now you can look after yourself."

Joe stared at him. His arms were covered in goosebumps from the cold already. He didn't even have a jacket to wear. He certainly wasn't prepared to face the wilderness in just a t-shirt.

"You want me to go back out there? On my own?" Joe asked.

"We've already done more for you than we needed to. We owe you nothing."

"Woah, hang on a second," the ginger girl said, stepping out of the house. "Let's not be hasty. Let's talk about this."

"What is there to talk about? He's a danger to us all."

"You can't just send him off on his own. He doesn't even have a weapon."

Luke gritted his teeth. "Ginge...this kid pointed a gun in our face the moment we laid eyes on him."

"I told you, it didn't have bullets in it! It was an antique!" Joe cried out, but Luke didn't even look his way as he cut him off.

"We have seen some shit out there today. This isn't a game. We're bloody lucky to have made it back here alive. He might be an idiot with an unloaded gun, or he might be someone who could actually get us killed. We can't take that risk."

Ginge stepped toward Luke. "Have you forgotten whose house this is?" she said sternly. Joe was pleased to see Luke squirm slightly in Ginge's presence. "This isn't just up to you. This is my house, and I get to decide who stays and who goes." Ginge turned toward Joe and looked him up and down. "But that's not to say that you get an automatic pass. What did you say your name was?"

"I'm...I'm Joe," he said nervously. Ginge nodded to him.

"Everyone calls me Ginge. This is my home. We haven't taken in any strangers before...but I'm not opposed to having more guests, provided they pull their weight. I don't want any free-riders.Tell me what happened back there, in your own words."

"He nearly-"

"Not you, Luke!" Ginge snapped. The six strangers in the yard turned to look at Joe. "Well? What have you got to say for yourself?"

Joe looked around at the strangers, feeling like a trapped animal in a cage. He could run, but then he'd be alone for good. He stared around at the hardened faces of his new acquaintances and felt his stomach twist.

"I was just trying to survive," Joe whispered. "I hadn't seen another person that wasn't one of...*them* all week. I don't know anyone in this town. So, when I saw these guys going into the house across the street...I figured my odds of survival would be better with a group than alone. But I made a mistake. I was careless. And Luke's right. I put their lives at risk. For that, I am sorry." Joe hung his head. "I don't know what I'm doing. It's clear you guys do. I'm sorry for causing you trouble. I understand why you want me to leave…but I can do better, I swear. I'm a good person. Sometimes not the smartest, sure…but I have skills. I could help you out around here." Joe nodded toward the barns. "I could help you keep your livestock safe. I can do odd jobs around the house. Hell, if you don't trust me, I can even build myself somewhere to stay, separate from you guys. I just…I don't want to survive this on my own anymore."

Luke continued to glare at Joe, but he saw the girls exchanging glances with one another. He took that to be a good sign. As scary as they seemed to him, they were only kids themselves - younger than he was. Now, with their weapons stowed and their hearts open, they didn't seem like the kind of people that would turn him away based on a mistake.

Or so he hoped.

"Thank you, Joe. I'm going to need to talk to my friends about this one, I think. It's my house, but my friends have a say in their safety too. Would you mind waiting out here while we all vote on what to do?"

"Of…of course," Joe said, hope rising inside him. He had so much to prove, so much to make up for already. But he was determined to make a second chance for himself.

He was determined to find himself somewhere to call home.

"I vote no."

"No surprises there," Heidi murmured to Rori at Luke's immediate response. The whole group was gathered in the kitchen, ready to vote on whether or not Joe should stay. Even Hannah and Billy had appeared for the discussion, eyes wide with curiosity. Rori was standing in the corner of the room, waiting to hear what everyone thought.

"Do you usually make a habit of inviting strangers into your home?" Luke snapped at Ginge. "I think this is ludicrous."

"Luke, he's only nineteen. He's been on his own through this whole thing, and he's clearly terrified. Now, I'm all for being careful, but I don't see how we can, in good conscience, send him out into the world alone. You brought him here yourself, and now he can't go back. If you send him out there, you're responsible for what happens to him next. And in all likelihood, it won't be a happy ending for him."

Luke opened his mouth to argue, but shut it again. It was clear to Rori that Luke didn't take well to strangers, but that he agreed with Ginge.

"You saved him from the horde for a reason," Ginge pointed out.

"Not wanting him dead and offering him sanctuary are two completely different things," Luke argued. Ginge crossed her arms, unconvinced.

"You guys took me and Rori in," Warren said quietly, catching Rori's eye across the room. "I don't know what would have happened to us if you hadn't."

"We knew you well enough," Luke argued. "You fought with us, proved yourselves. All Joe has done is bring us trouble."

"To be fair, he could say the same about us," Rori pointed out. "Us showing up brought all the rotters to the yard. Everything was going swimmingly in his life before Luke threw him into the trunk of our car."

"I saved his life. It wouldn't have needed saving if he hadn't caused a scene," Luke insisted. He turned back to Ginge. "Look. We don't know this guy. What if he's some kind of psycho? He could have lied to us about who he is."

Ginge sighed. "I get what you're saying, Luke, I really do. You forget I have my siblings to protect, so I'm not about to do anything to put them in harm's way. But he seems like a normal guy. Just someone who got unlucky, I suppose. I think he could be useful to us. I could use some extra manpower around the farm. You guys are great, but I'm the only one who really knows what they're doing when it comes to running this place. I don't see any harm in giving him a trial run here. We can keep an eye on him, make sure that he's not going to cause any trouble. And then we can take it from there."

Everyone in the room began to murmur in what sounded like agreement. It seemed like a sensible plan to Rori, but from the thunderous look on Luke's face, the idea didn't sit well with all members of the group.

"I think it's a huge mistake," Luke said darkly. Ginge looked around at her friends.

"I think it's a small risk. One I'm willing to take. We don't know how many survivors there are left. Joe might be one of only a few. If that's the case, then we need to stick together. We need to fight together, not against one another. I say that we let him stay a week, see what he can do. He can get his hands dirty, show us that he's not going to get us all killed. And then in a week, we can vote again."

"I've got to say, I'm with Ginge," Cassie said, glancing nervously at Luke. Due to being logical and mostly sensible, it was rare that Cassie and Luke ever disagreed on something, but for once, they were at odds. "I know he made a stupid mistake…but haven't we all made mistakes? We all let Gemma wander off on her own and she got herself killed. Now we're all here, still alive, together. We learned and we moved forward. Doesn't Joe deserve the chance to do the same?"

"It was me who nearly died because of him, and I'm game to give him another chance," Heidi said with a shrug. "If I had a pound for every time I messed up, I'd be rich as hell. Not that it would mean much anymore, but you get the point. I vote to let him stay, for now."

"Me too," Cassie said with a decisive nod.

"Raise your hand if you're in favor?" Ginge said, avoiding Luke's gaze. One by one, everyone else in the room raised their hand aside from Luke. He threw his hands up in frustration and headed straight for the door.

"Fine. But don't come crying to me when he gets us all killed."

Chapter Eight

"Stay with me," Charlie pleaded. Tears streamed down his face as he cradled Nora's head in his hands. The wound in her shoulder was deep and blood was seeping from it fast. Too fast. "Nora, stay with me. I've got you."

"Charlie," Nora breathed. Her eyes were stricken, like she couldn't quite process what was happening. Fletcher's throat was tight. They all knew that an injury like hers was a death sentence. It was the disease that would kill her, not the wound.

"I'm here," Charlie whispered, pressing his forehead to her's. Nora's lip wobbled.

"I can't believe I was always such a bitch to you."

Charlie smiled through his tears. "I wouldn't have it any other way."

"You're not so bad, really."

"That might be the kindest thing you've ever said to me."

Nora laughed softly, but her eyes kept fluttering shut. Her chest rose and fell with each shuddering breath. Her skin was pasty as the disease moved through her body. It was all happening so fast. It was clear that Nora wouldn't take long to turn.

Charlie looked up suddenly, as if remembering that Patrick and Fletcher were there. "Patrick," he hissed urgently, through sobs. "Patrick, you can do something. She's dying. You've got to do something. Please."

Patrick swallowed. All he could bring himself to do was shake his head.

"Charlie, no," Nora whispered. She opened her eyes to meet Charlie's, as if telling him that there was nothing he could do. She tried to smile at him. "It's okay."

"No…it's not. It's not okay. It'll never be okay."

Charlie took a shuddering breath, putting a hand over the wound on Nora's shoulder to stop the flow of blood. "It should have been me," he whispered. "Why couldn't you let it be me?"

"I couldn't lose you," Nora said simply.

Charlie opened his mouth to speak, but all that came out was a sob. He brushed the dark curls off Nora's forehead gently with bloodied hands. Her breathing was starting to slow.

"*Nora*!" Charlie shouted. The cry ripped harshly through his throat. Fletcher didn't even worry that the noise would attract more Zeds. All he felt was numb, watching blood gush from the wound on Nora's shoulder.

When it was time, Patrick knelt beside Nora and gently closed her eyes. Charlie was kneeling before her, his head bowed over her as if in prayer, his hands slick with her blood.

It took all of Patrick and Fletcher's strength to drag Charlie away from her body.

"We can't leave her," Charlie argued. He fought against their hold. "We've got to go back for her…we can't leave her there."

But there was nothing to be done. Fletcher knew that now. Their priority was keeping Charlie safe. He locked eyes with Patrick, and a silent agreement passed between them. For Nora, they needed to keep him safe.

Fletcher barely registered the walk from the town back up to the school. How could they return when their group was one fewer? When they had lost the most spirited, confident member of their team? And how could they manage to convince everyone else at the school that leaving was their best option when they had Nora's blood on their hands?

Their journey was silent out of respect for Nora, save for an occasional sob from Charlie. What words could be shared that would bear the weight of their loss? The Zeds that did cross their path, Charlie was quick to dispatch off, turning his pain into aggression against the monsters that had cost him so much.

It was Patrick who finally broke the silence. They had reached the school gates, and all seemed eerily quiet. "Look, over there," Patrick said to Fletcher. He pointed with a shaking hand to the athletics field around the back of the school. Squinting against the autumn sunlight, Fletcher spotted a mass of figures behind the school fences, ant-like in their united movement.

A wall of Zeds, headed straight for the school. Patrick took a shuddering breath.

"If we weren't fucked before, we are now."

Zoe was waiting for them on the other side of the cafeteria doors, pacing. Fletcher got the impression that she hadn't left her post at the door once since they'd left. She ushered them in, her face a picture of relief. That was, until she saw the sorry looks on each of the three boys' faces.

Her eyebrows furrowed in confusion when she realized they were only a party of three. She poked her head out into the corridor, searching left and right.

"Patrick," Zoe said, a tremor of panic in her voice. "Patrick, where's Nora? Is she alright?"

Patrick shook his head in response, his shoulders slumped. "She..." he cleared his throat. "She got bitten. There was nothing we could do."

Zoe covered her mouth with her hand. Her brown eyes were wide with shock as she absorbed the information. Fletcher still couldn't quite believe it himself. He kept expecting to hear Nora's sassy remarks at Charlie's expense, or see a sly smile spreading on her face.

But there was only heavy silence.

"Charlie, I...I'm so sorry," Zoe said. She put a hand on his arm consolingly.

A small cough interrupted their respectful silence. In his grief, Fletcher hadn't spotted that there was a new face amongst those in the cafeteria. The newcomer was a few years older than Fletcher - perhaps the same age as Charlie - and there was arrogance in the nonchalant way he slumped against the wall and coughed for attention.

"Oh, don't mind me," said the boy. The man had deep brown eyes and floppy brown hair, like he was from an old boy band that everyone had forgotten about.

"I'm sorry," Charlie said. He squared up to the newcomer, rolling his shoulders back. Fletcher looked nervously at Patrick and Zoe. They had sensed the same thing. Charlie was clearly not in the mood to be tested. "But who the fuck are you?"

"I'm Ross."

"Well, Ross," Charlie said. "We just lost someone out there, so if you could be a bit more sensitive, that would be great." His voice dripped with sarcasm.

"Of course." Ross smiled. Fletcher thought he looked like a fox when he smiled.

"She sacrificed herself to save me," Charlie told Zoe. His eyes welled with tears. "It should have been me."

"There wasn't anything you could have done, mate," Patrick said to Charlie, putting a hand consolingly on his broad shoulder. "It all happened so quickly…none of us could have anticipated it. We just got unlucky. Really unlucky."

Charlie shrugged Patrick's hand off his shoulder, clearly needing a moment to compose himself. Zoe grappled for something to say, even as her eyes filled with unshed tears.

"The new kid…Ross. He just showed up, shortly before you did. He was terrified, so I let him in. He's on his own, or so he says."

"Great. Just what we need. More people to help," Charlie muttered. "And an asshole at that."

"Let us handle this," Zoe told Charlie gently. "You've done enough today."

Zoe looked at Patrick and nodded. Their silent communication had Patrick moving into the center of the room, his head held high. Fletcher knew that Charlie was in no fit state to lead the group, and that his grief wouldn't fill anyone with confidence, but it felt wrong for Patrick to take his place, somehow. Wrong for him to take Nora's too.

"Alright, listen up," Patrick called out to the room. "We've scouted out the town. It looks like a load of survivors banded together at the town hall. They aren't there anymore, but we have an idea of where they're headed." Patrick looked at Fletcher. "Some of them left messages for us, before they left. Parents, friends, family. There could be messages there for any of us. We think it's worth making a move there. It seems like our best shot."

There was a murmur around the room at this point. Some young faces looked hopeful; others hesitant to believe what they were being told. Fletcher knew they'd need more convincing to consider leaving the safety of the school.

"Where's Nora?" Colin piped up.

"She er..." Patrick hesitated. "Unfortunately, she was attacked by a Zed."

Colin blinked. "She's...she's gone?"

Patrick bowed his head. "Yes. It was...it was hard to see. But it couldn't have been prevented."

"You didn't *have* to go out there, right? Surely she'd still be alive if she'd stayed behind?" Ross pointed out, raising a smug eyebrow. Charlie's anger seemed to flare up again, but Zoe held his wrist to keep him back, giving him a warning glance.

"It isn't safe out there," one kid said, and she was supported by a ripple of agreement. "If Nora couldn't make it, we can't either."

"I know you're all freaked about Nora," Fletcher said, casting a nervous glance at Charlie. "We are too. She was the strongest of us. But, she didn't want us to stay here and wait around to die. She risked her life to prove that there's more to this than just surviving. I

83

owe it to her - we all do - to her memory, to find a life that's worth living out there."

Ross stepped forward, facing Fletcher, Patrick, Zoe and Charlie as if opposing them. He turned to the younger kids. "Just because his girlfriend died-"

Patrick sprung forwards as Charlie lunged at Ross. Ross squirmed away just in time, but there was an ugly, smug expression on his face. He clearly knew he was goading Charlie, and he was enjoying it.

"I don't know who the fuck you think you are," Charlie hissed. "But if you *ever* talk about her again-"

"Let's just hope your right-hand man will always be around to stop you from doing something stupid," Ross said, his eyes sizing up Patrick.

"Look," Patrick said, desperately trying to stop things from getting out of hand. Clearly, this proposal wasn't going as smoothly as he'd intended. "This isn't *just* about Nora or your families. There's also a horde of Zeds on their way straight to the school. Too many for us to fight." He didn't need to point out that they were even more outnumbered now that Nora was gone.

"The school has gates," Ross argued. He looked at the younger students. "You've survived here for this long. It's been safe…why leave now?"

"You can't stay," Fletcher tried his best to implore. "Sure, you've got gates. But we know the Zeds. They will find a way to get in. They always do."

"There's food here! And we have the barricades," Colin said, his voice trembling. "We don't have to fight here…"

"Because Nora and I have always been around to save you," Charlie snapped. "And now I'm telling you that you'll die if you stay here."

The room fell quiet for a moment. No one had ever seen this side of Charlie before. He was broken. Unhinged. He wasn't the leader they'd come to know, not in that moment.

And suddenly, Ross was stepping forward.

"You know what? I think most of us will take our chances here," Ross said, glancing around the room. "We know where the grass is greener. I'd say this is our best shot."

"And why should anyone trust you? You've been here five minutes and you've already managed to piss everyone off," Charlie growled. Ross shrugged slowly.

"I'm simply agreeing with what everyone here thinks. It's crazy to go out there. Believe me, I've seen it. I had to run once, but I'm not doing that again. This is the real deal." Ross folded his arms across his chest. "No one's stopping you from leaving, right? Let people make their own decisions. No one needs you to play the dictator."

Charlie's eyes were filled with fire. Fletcher could see that the anger inside him was about to consume him. He was scared of what he might do if he tipped over the edge.

But he unclenched his fist. Slowly, quietly, the fight left his body. It was like he was questioning why he even fought for the others in the first place. He'd been their beacon of hope in their darkest hour. And yet, no one seemed to have a shred of faith in him.

Charlie turned his back on the students silently, moving to collect his bag. Zoe wavered.

"Charlie...let's talk about this."

"No. I'm done. If they want to stay, let them," Charlie said, his voice trembling with anger. He turned his back on the students, his expression dark. "Nora was right. Come on guys, we're done baby-sitting."

It didn't take long to gather their belongings and bid their farewells to the other students. Ross had managed to scare the younger kids into believing they were safer staying in the school, and no amount of convincing on Fletcher, Patrick or Zoe's behalf could change their minds. It only made matters worse that Charlie barely said a word. Fletcher could see that the fight had gone out of him, and he didn't blame Charlie for his lack of enthusiasm at the prospect of a life without Nora.

The four of them headed out into the parking lot, not looking back at what they were leaving behind. They were silent as they walked towards the ambulance that Zoe and Patrick had arrived on site in. Fletcher had never been in an ambulance before, but it didn't excite him now. He just hoped that the vehicle would be strong enough to keep them safe from the Zeds.

Zoe drove the ambulance in silence, quietly navigating them away from the school. Charlie was slumped in the front seat next to her. He'd pulled his hood up around his face, as if blocking out as much of the world as he could. Fletcher and Patrick rode together in the back with all of their supplies. Their weapons were in the back too; Fletcher was starting to get attached to his javelin. It wasn't the comfiest ride in the world, but the ambulance felt safer than a car, at least.

Fletcher was glad to leave the school behind, but he was scared. They'd lost one member of their group today; he wasn't sure he'd ever be ready to lose another one.

He didn't know where they were headed, or if they'd ever find what they were looking for, and it made the world ahead of them seem so incredibly expansive. Their plan to find the national park had died with Nora, seeing as she had their map, and now, they had no route to take. Fletcher shuddered to himself, wishing he knew how their journey was going to pan out.

"That guy, Ross," Fletcher said. He wanted to break the silence. He could feel Nora's absence. He could even imagine her, shot-gunning the front seat of the ambulance next to Zoe. She'd be leaning back with her feet propped up on the dashboard, throwing out sarcastic remarks about a "road-trip" as she fiddled with the stereo. "What happened there?"

"He just showed up out of the blue," Zoe said. Zoe indicated as she took a left turn out of habit. "When he turned up at the cafeteria, he looked terrified. And he was *covered* in blood. I thought he must have run into some trouble…and I took pity on him. But the minute he got into the cafeteria, the fear fell away. I don't want to say it was an act, but it was like he switched. I can't put my finger on it, but there was definitely something about him that changed the minute I let him inside. Maybe it's because he realized it was just me with a bunch of kids, and he didn't see me as a threat. He definitely bristled when you two arrived though," she added, looking at Patrick and Charlie.

"We do make an intimidating duo," Patrick said, cracking his knuckles as if to emphasize the point. It was a half-hearted attempt at a joke, and Fletcher could tell that Patrick's heart wasn't really in it.

"It was odd though…he didn't really have much of a story. He didn't mention being with any other survivors. Maybe it's just me, but I'm not sure I trust anyone who's survived this long on their own. It makes me wonder what they might have done to get so far without any help." Zoe shuddered. "I'm sorry for letting him in…maybe that's too trusting of me. But I didn't really know what to do, and I genuinely thought he was scared."

Patrick reached forwards and squeezed Zoe's shoulder comfortingly as she drove. Zoe managed a small smile at him in the rear-view mirror.

"You did what any of us would have done," Patrick assured her. "We don't know how many survivors are left; he's one of the first we've met. Just a shame that he seems like an insufferable knob." Patrick took a glug of his water. "That doesn't mean we shouldn't be wary of who we meet, but it's innocent until proven guilty as far as I'm concerned."

"But we don't know the things these people have done to survive," Charlie added darkly.

This sentiment hung heavily in the air between them. Charlie was right. Even within their group, they'd all done horrific acts that, a week earlier, they didn't realize they were capable of. And there would be people out there who had done much worse, Fletcher was sure of it. People who might have turned their violent hands from Zeds to their fellow survivors.

People who might have killed.

"From now on," Zoe decided. "The only people we can trust are each other."

She pulled the ambulance into a parking space in a lot by a fast food chain. It struck Fletcher how odd it felt to be doing something as mundane as using a parking space when the world had changed so much.

"First stop, town hall," Zoe announced. "Let's split up and see what we can find inside. Maybe we can find another map to get to the national park." She checked her mirror. "The coast is clear, guys."

Patrick opened the back of the ambulance, and he and Fletcher hopped down onto the tarmac. Fletcher reached back inside for his trusty javelin while Zoe locked the ambulance, and the four of them set off towards the town square. They took a narrow alley towards the clock tower. It wasn't the same one as they'd taken with Nora, but it was similar enough to send shivers up Fletcher's spine. With the high walls either side of him and dumpsters pushed up against the walls, he suddenly felt claustrophobic.

"Can you hear that sound?" Zoe asked nervously. She seemed on edge.

Fletcher paused. The sound was a distant hum, almost like a generator or a wind tunnel. He was about to communicate this observation, when the alley swung to the left and the source of the noise greeted them.

88

Zeds were pouring down the alley ahead of them.

Patrick, at the front of the group, turned quickly. He motioned with his hand to the others to turn around, not wanting to draw any more attention to them. Now, it seemed clear where all the Zeds had disappeared to earlier that day. It was like they had gotten themselves trapped and not bothered to try and get out with no active targets to aim for. Fletcher wanted nothing more than to get away from them.

But when they turned, they were met by another horde of Zeds approaching the alley entrance from the way they'd just come from.

They were trapped.

Heart racing, Fletcher looked around the alley for a hiding place. The dumpsters were big enough for them to hide in, and the rubbish could mask their smell, but Fletcher feared they'd be waiting a long time for the horde to pass, especially since it seemed to have been stagnant for a while. To his right, Patrick seemed to reach the same conclusion, but as he turned to consult Fletcher, Patrick's eyes widened.

"That ladder by the vent," Patrick said quickly. "It's a fire escape. We can wait it out up there."

Zoe was nearest the ladder. Her trainers slid on the rungs in her hurry to ascend. Patrick followed her quickly. Fletcher stood at the bottom of the ladder next to a dumpster, ready to follow them up. He looked around him.

Where was Charlie?

"Charlie!" Fletcher called in a half whisper.

Charlie was standing in the center of the narrow walkway, surrounded by litter and abandoned bin bags. He was eyeing up the Zeds that had started ambling down the alley with a look of pure loathing on his face. He tossed his baseball bat from hand to hand, as if readying for combat.

"Charlie!" Fletcher repeated his name. "You're crazy if you think you can fight them. There's too many!"

"They killed Nora," Charlie snarled.

Fletcher grabbed Charlie's arm. "I know they killed her," he said. "And I know you're upset, and you're angry. But now isn't the time. She wouldn't want you to die trying to avenge her. That's no way to honor her sacrifice."

He knew it was a low blow, but it seemed to do the trick. Fletcher took advantage of Charlie's moment of hesitation to push the older boy towards the fire escape ladder.

Charlie was quick, scaling the ladder with ease. Fletcher wasted no time in trying to follow him, grabbing rung after rung in quick succession. Too quick.

He felt his hands slip on the metal rungs of the ladder. A hand clamped on his ankle from below and he kicked out desperately. The hand returned to its owner, but the kick had set Fletcher off balance. He lost his grip, and he swung around so that his back crashed against the wall, his fingers barely managing to hold on. Suspended over the hungry crowd below, his trainers dangled just out of their reach.

Fletcher felt his grip loosening.

A strong hand closed around his wrist. Charlie. Noticing his struggle, the older boy had scaled down the rungs to his assistance.

"Hold on!" Charlie said.

He pulled Fletcher back towards the ladder. Fletcher slipped his trainers between the rungs again, ignoring the weakness in his knees and his racing heart. When he felt steady, Charlie slowly let go of his wrist and Fletcher clung to the ladder. He needed a moment to catch his breath.

For a moment, he thought he was done for.

"Thanks," Fletcher panted. His t-shirt was damp with sweat. He wanted to wipe his hair out of his eyes, but he didn't dare let go of the ladder again.

"Don't mention it," Charlie said. "You did me a solid back there, kid. I've got you."

Fletcher started climbing, slower this time. He was out of reach of the Zeds, but that didn't mean he was safe.

"It's a dead end!" Zoe called down to them. She'd raced along the fire escape ahead of them, and was pushing against the fire door at the end with her shoulder.

The hungry moans of the Zeds below were deafening. Their hands clawed greedily towards the sky, to the tempting meal trapped on the fire escape balcony above them. Fletcher tried to ignore them as he climbed, taking each rung one cautious step at a time. He really didn't want to slip again and fall toward the gaping jaws of the undead.

Once he was on the landing, Patrick and Charlie started to pull the metal ladder up. They hadn't seen any evidence that the Zeds could climb, but they weren't in any hurry to test that theory. Fletcher scurried past Patrick and Charlie to help Zoe with the door.

Together, they pushed against the door. Fletcher felt pain blossom over his shoulder as he rammed it against the metal. Getting desperate, he aimed a kick at the door, sending a painful shudder up his leg.

"That wasn't a good idea, was it?" Zoe said.

"No," Fletcher winced, leaning on his other foot.

He shrank back against the fire door. He didn't want to see the Zeds below. He wondered if they would ever lose interest in them. He closed his eyes, racing through escape scenarios in his head, each more ridiculous than the last.

That was when he heard a metal bolt slide on the other side of the door.

The door gave way.

Fletcher cried out as rough hands hauled him away backwards into the darkness.

Chapter Nine

Luke had places he'd rather be than on the night watch with Joe, but that was where he had wound up. It had been a few days since he'd been brought to the farm, and Luke wasn't any less wary of him, despite Joe's best efforts to prove himself. He'd been running around the farm doing odd jobs, fortifying their windows with wood panels, taking every watch he could, and even helping with the cooking. The others appeared to be warming to him, glad to have an extra pair of hands around the farm, but Luke couldn't shake the feeling that they were making a big mistake allowing Joe to stay with them.

Sure, he looked innocent from the outside, with his goofy smile and his bright blue eyes. Sure, he was polite and useful and he hadn't caused a single issue since his arrival. In a bid to win him over, Joe had even asked Luke if he'd fancied a game of chess.

But at the back of his mind, Luke could still see the rotter diving at Heidi, so close to tearing her throat out. He could still see Joe standing on the staircase with the pistol pointed at him. He could still feel the way his heart flailed as they ran out to the car to escape the rotters, all because of Joe.

And now, he was clinging to those memories. He didn't want to forget that Joe wasn't someone he could trust and rely on.

He could sense that Joe was uncomfortable around him, too. Luke had made his stance clear, avoiding talking to Joe if he could. He saw no point in Joe getting comfortable, anyway. After his week's trial, Luke was intending to ask him to go on his way. Surely then his friends would back him up?

"Can you see Orion's belt up ahead?" Joe said, his voice forcefully cheerful. Luke was sure he was the last person Joe wanted to be on the night watch with too, but he had a determined smile on his face. Luke rolled his eyes.

"It's the easiest constellation in the sky to spot. Of course I can see it. Shouldn't you be concentrating on keeping watch?"

Joe's shoulders slumped a little. "You're right. Sorry."

The pair of them fell back into silence. Luke didn't care. He was built to withstand uncomfortable silences better than most. He saw no point in mindless chatter that didn't go anywhere, even if that meant saying nothing at all. He didn't want to chat with Joe, anyway. That meant that there was a stronger possibility of finding good inside him, of warming to his presence, and that was the last thing that Luke needed.

But Joe didn't seem keen to let the tension between them stay. He was making an obvious attempt to catch Luke's eye in the darkness, but Luke simply gritted his teeth, staring ahead of him with determination. That usually deterred most people.

But not Joe.

"Look, Luke…I know you don't like me much. You've made that clear."

"What makes you think that?" Luke asked dryly. Joe sighed.

"Your friends don't seem to feel so harshly toward me. I think maybe they've managed to forgive me for what happened the other day."

"Good for them."

Joe was doing his best to be patient, so he didn't sigh, but Luke knew he wanted to. He had mastered the art of being difficult to reach emotionally. He was certain that Joe wasn't about to break down any barriers any time soon.

"I used to have a good group of friends back home, you know, back in Glasgow. A group kind of like yours. So I'm not totally unbearable, I know that much."

"Could have fooled me. Besides, why should I believe that just because you tell me it's true? It's like giving yourself a five star

94

review and awarding yourself Person of the Year. Doesn't have much credibility."

Joe chewed his lip. "You've really got an answer for everything, haven't you?"

"I like to think so."

Joe paused again. Their conversation felt like a minefield. Like one of them was going to explode at any moment.

"You know what I thought, after the one person I knew in this town turned?" Joe asked quietly. "Bear in mind, I'm miles from anyone I know. I couldn't phone my parents, my friends...I even thought about calling my ex, to be honest. I was desperate for some human connection. But the phones have been down this whole time, and I was alone. And I felt that. So I thought...I thought that I might never see a living person again. I was too scared to venture out alone, unarmed...I thought that I'd just stay in that house until I died. I don't know if you understand what that's like. You guys had each other from the start. But I was completely alone."

Luke stayed quiet, staring out at the fields ahead of them, but he was listening. Because Joe was right. He didn't understand his situation.

He was interested to know what his excuses for his behavior were.

Joe sighed, shrugging his shoulders. "When I saw you guys...I saw hope. I saw a chance to live. That was the only thing on my mind. I took my grandfather's gun and walked out of that house without even closing the door behind me. Without even looking back at what I was leaving for a chance with you guys. I didn't look out for danger. It was like I could barely see, barely hear. All I could focus on was the possibility that I might make it out alive if I just got to you guys. I guess that's how the rotter got inside. Because of me." Joe hung his head. "If anything bad had happened...if it had turned out for the worst...I never would have forgiven myself.

But…but we're all still alive. We all made it through. And I think I've proved that I can be useful. I think the others can see that I'm not a bad person. But you don't see it that way, do you?"

Luke closed his eyes for a brief moment. "I'm no stranger to human error. You might think me harsh, Joe, but I was just trying to protect the people I care about." He opened his eyes again, keeping his gaze on the perimeter. "People think I don't care. That I don't give a shit about anyone, but myself. And it's not true at all. Just because I don't act like everything is unicorns and rainbows, everyone thinks I'm cold." He turned to look at Joe. "But the one thing I've been trying to do since all of this began is stop these idiots I call my friends from dying. They don't seem to be able to grasp that, and maybe you don't either. I don't trust you because you're not one of us, Joe. You could be the nicest guy on Earth, but I don't know you, and I'm not out here trying to make friends. I'm trying to survive, and I'd rather that my friends were with me while I do that. You get it?"

Joe nodded silently.

"The only reason I haven't been more vocal about you staying here is because I can't, in good conscience, send anyone out there alone. From what I've seen, no one can last a day alone on the streets. There are more rotters than ever, and once you turn, that's it. The balance between humans and rotters is tipping more every day, and not in our favor. But don't think for a second that means I want you here. You pointed a gun at me. You brought trouble to our doorstep. And sure, things are fine now, but what about when they're not anymore? What happens when you let us down next? I guess I'll say I told you so to those of my friends that survive that ordeal."

Joe looked so hurt that Luke had to look away again. He didn't want to cut Joe apart with his words, but he was just trying to be honest. Joe took a shaky breath.

"If I had any choice, I'd go elsewhere," Joe whispered. "I don't want to impose on your life. I don't want to get in the way. But my options are to stay here or die. So I'm not going anywhere. I'll keep my head down, I'll work hard…maybe someday there will be a way out of this and we can go our separate ways. But until then, I guess you'll just have to get used to me."

Luke stared at Joe, who was now doing his best to look anywhere, but at him. He hadn't expected him to have the backbone to talk to Luke like that. At least that was something he could admire. But that was where his fondness for Joe ended, and he planned to keep it that way.

He couldn't have anyone thinking he might have been wrong about Joe.

"Hey."

Cassie shuffled into the kitchen. Her blonde hair was still damp from the shower, and it spilled over the shoulders of the baggy sweatshirt she'd pulled on.

Poppy smiled at her friend. "Hey, you. Staying out of trouble?"

"If by that you mean staying out of Luke's way," Cassie said. "Yes, yes I am."

Cassie grabbed a clean tea towel and started helping Poppy wipe the dishes from their meager meal. It was small gestures like these that Poppy appreciated most about her friend. Cassie never made her feel like it was a chore to help, or that she needed thanking for it.

"What do you think about Joe?" Poppy asked. "You were there when he approached you. I trust what you say."

Cassie thought about it for a moment. "He didn't set himself up well," she mused. "It's not a great impression to make of yourself when you're holding a literal gun, loaded or not. But he was scared, you could see the fear in his eyes. And when you're scared, you don't think rationally. We do need to be careful. We can't trust people the way that we have in the past. It brings out an ugly side to us all. We're tired, we're hungry, we probably smell really bad and we're in constant fear. None of us are at our best when we're just trying to survive."

"But Luke seems so against the idea of trusting him," Poppy said.

"I think Luke is frustrated more than anything," Cassie said. She and Luke were close and they'd always held a mutual respect for one another. That meant something when it came to Luke. He didn't let people in easily. "And I get it, I really do. Something as simple as leaving a door open can mean the difference between life and death now. But Luke is logical. If he sees that Joe can be an asset to our group, he'll come around. He didn't warm to Rori or Warren at first, but they proved themselves. Joe just needs to go above and beyond that to make up for pointing a gun at us."

"What if we're just being really naive, thinking we can trust an outsider?"

Cassie shrugged. "If we are being naive, we'll know not to make the same mistake again. It's not like he can stab us in the back when we're all so close. We'd take him down before he got the chance. I still think that we need to give people a chance. If we don't have our humanity, what separates us from the rotters?"

"Sometimes I envy them; the rotters. They don't have to go through all of this," Poppy said quietly. Cassie frowned, putting a hand gently on Poppy's arm.

"What's going on?" she asked. She had developed an annoying knack of being able to read her best friend. Poppy often thought that Cassie knew how she felt before she even knew what she was feeling.

"I'm fine," Poppy lied defensively. Why did people keep thinking she wasn't?

"Okay."

Cassie didn't say anything more. It was a tactic that infuriated Poppy, but it always seemed to work. She always gave in and talked eventually.

"I don't know what I'm doing here, Cass," Poppy admitted quietly. Her eyes felt tired, and so she pushed her glasses onto the top of her head. "You and the others are fighting for our lives, keeping us safe. What am I doing? Scrubbing pots and pans and cleaning up everyone else's mess."

"I can ask everyone to be a bit tidier- "

"This isn't about that!" Poppy snapped. Cassie flinched, and Poppy immediately felt guilty as Cassie stepped back defensively. She took a deep breath.

"I'm sorry," she apologized. She squeezed Cassie's arm. She hadn't meant to snap. Here Cassie was, trying to help, and all she could do was find flaws in her solutions. "Everything is so intense and all I feel is useless."

"You're not useless," Cassie said, shaking her head. She moved closer subconsciously, and Poppy was overly aware of their proximity in the large kitchen. She could smell the shampoo that Cassie had used and almost feel the shower warmth radiating from her skin.

"Everyone else has found a place where they belong out here. Eliza and Heidi have each other; Ginge has the farm to take care of, and her siblings; Luke's on his own, but he's always liked it that way. What do I have?"

"You've got all of us," Cassie said, frowning. "You're not just cleaning up everyone's mess."

Poppy rolled her eyes and flicked her tea towel at the clean dishes piled on the draining board. Cassie nodded.

"Okay; physically, there is a mess," Cassie admitted. "And you do a great job of cleaning that up. But figuratively…it's not just about cleaning things up and keeping things tidy. It's about having somewhere that's worth protecting. It's about having a home.

Making it feel like a place we want to be, that we want to protect. And maybe this place feels like home because we've been here so many times before. Or maybe it feels like home because we've got great memories here. But maybe it feels like home to me because you're here, making it a better place."

Poppy raised her eyes to Cassie's. Cassie blushed and tugged her eyes away from Poppy's.

"Look," Cassie continued. "We can go out and fight rotters all we like, but what's the point if we don't have anywhere to go to in the end? What are we doing this all for, if not for a home and a place in the world?"

"I get that," Poppy said. "I do… it just feels like such a passive role."

"You can come with us," Cassie suggested. "There will be more runs. Luke would have a fit, but he needs to get over it, to be honest."

Poppy smiled. "I don't want to give Luke a heart attack," she said. "And it's not like I really want to be out there fighting. I know that's not my strength. I just sometimes feel…lost?"

"I get it." Cassie leant back against the kitchen worktop, looking down at her feet. "I feel lost too. I'm used to having an annoying little brother to look out for all the time."

"…now you've just got an annoying best friend having an existential crisis," Poppy finished.

"It's an apocalypse; I'd be concerned if you *weren't* having an existential crisis."

"You just seem so calm and collected all the time," Poppy said. "You act like nothing fazes you and you know what you're doing. You're strong, and everyone looks to you for stability. You act like you belong."

"Poppy, I don't know what I'm doing either," Cassie said. "When I'm fighting rotters, all I let myself think of is how to survive it. But I'd rather be fighting them than not. The more you face your fears, the less scary they become, I suppose."

"There's that saying…keep your friends close and your enemies closer."

"Exactly. It's not pleasant getting all up in the rotters' business…but each time I do it, it reminds me that I'm stronger. That we all are. I need to know that. It's the only thing that means I can actually sleep at night."

Cassie fell quiet. They'd all struggled to sleep. It was getting easier, but Poppy was yet to sleep without dreams plagued by rotters. She'd wake in the night suddenly, her heart racing and adrenaline pumping as the image of clawing, rotting hands started to fade. Half-asleep, Cassie would reach across to her in the darkness and Poppy would hold onto her until her breathing returned to normal.

"It was hard today," Poppy admitted after a while. She'd turned her back to Cassie as she put clean glasses away in the cupboards, but she could feel Cassie looking at her. "It's so hard watching you go out there and not knowing if you'll make it back."

"I know you worry about us," Cassie said. "But we trust our instincts. They haven't let us down before."

Poppy turned to face her friend. Her eyes flicked between Cassie's. "It's hard watching all of you go, but it's hardest letting *you* go."

Cassie took a deep breath. "It's hard saying goodbye," she replied. "I worry about what I'm going to come back to, whether the farm has been overrun. But I came back, didn't I?"

"What if there's a time that you don't?" Poppy whispered. "What happens then?"

"I don't know, Pops," Cassie sighed. "I don't know."

Cassie brushed her hand against Poppy's cheek gently before pulling her into a hug. Poppy buried her face against Cassie's neck, breathing in her familiar scent. She wanted to stay like that, wrapped in the comfort of Cassie's embrace, forgetting about the rotters and the bloodshed of the past days. She felt safe with Cassie. Cassie knew the ugliest and weakest parts of her that Poppy tried to hide from everyone else. She needed that.

"I need some sleep," Cassie said wearily when they finally pulled apart. "You coming?"

"Yeah, I'll just…I've just got some stuff to do," Poppy said. "You go up, don't wait around for me."

She watched Cassie head off to use the bathroom, leaving Poppy wondering whether it was just the world around them that was changing.

Chapter Ten

Rori's heart was granted relief from the moment he clambered up into the attic. He'd been on high alert for so long that it felt like he might never settle down again. But the thought of a full night's sleep and the safety of the upper floor made him feel as close to comfort as he was ever going to get again.

Heidi was already up there, getting herself ready for sleep. She had bagged herself a space in the corner on their first night at the farm, and Rori had taken to sleeping beside her. At first, it was because she was the closest thing he had to a friend. Now, he stayed because he felt safer beside her. He'd seen the way she fought when they were out there together, like she would do anything to protect the group. And whenever he felt his heart seize, whenever he feared that it was all about to be over, she seemed to be right there beside him, guarding his back.

She was in the process of wrestling with her sleeping bag to get in a comfortable position. It was early, only just before sundown, but they'd been up most of the previous night on watch, and Rori was bone tired. Still, he liked to chat a while with Heidi most nights before they went to sleep.

"I miss my bed," she grumbled. "That was my happy place, I swear. Any opportunity I had to be in bed, I would be. I'd read in bed, sleep too late in an attempt to skip college, get into my pajamas the moment I arrived home from anywhere…and now it just isn't the same. I can feel a spring poking in my back all night, and Ginge didn't have a single pair of fluffy socks for me to sleep in. I'm losing my sanity."

"I thought you already lost that?" Rori said with an easy smile as he sat down beside her, trying to make himself comfortable on the old mattress. It was made more difficult by the lumps beneath him and he wriggled around a little.

"You're hardly helping matters, encouraging all of my worst behaviors. It's like having a male version of myself joined at my hip."

Rori managed a smile, but it was a weak one. He often felt fatigue wash over him from the moment he made it to the attic. It was like all of the pressure of the day was taken off him, leaving his body bruised and battered, as well as his mind.

"Hey…are you alright?" Heidi asked, cocking her head to the side. Rori leaned his back against the wall, averting his eyes.

"Yeah, I'm fine."

"It's just that I think you're bullshitting me. You've been quiet ever since we went on the scouting trip the other day. And I know you don't sleep well."

"How do you know?"

Heidi smiled softly. "Because I don't either. When I'm lying awake every night, I hear you tossing and turning, and I always want to just reach over and let you know that I'm wide awake too. But I think better of it most nights."

Rori felt a small smile dragging at the corner of his lips. It was nice to think that he wasn't alone, though he didn't like the thought of Heidi suffering in unison. He forced his shoulders to relax a little.

"What keeps you awake?"

Heidi shrugged. "Oh you know, the usual. The sound of rotters outside. Wondering if my family is out there somewhere, still alive, maybe even searching for me and Eliza..." She paused. "The memory of what I did to Toby."

Rori's forehead creased into a frown. "You didn't *do* anything."

"Maybe that's the point. I didn't do enough," Heidi said quietly. She glanced up at Rori. "Logically, I know I did everything I could. But I lie awake at night and there's this little voice in my head saying…what if? What if? What if I hadn't fucked up?" Heidi shook her head to herself. "I hear him scream. Every single night. And I think about the fact that if we'd been a few moments faster, then he

104

might still be here now. Annoying the hell out of us, most likely." Heidi paused, and there was a wobble in her voice. "And I don't think I'll ever be able to stop thinking about that."

Rori couldn't think of a single thing to say. What could you possibly say to comfort that kind of grief? Heidi sucked in air and forced a smile, like they'd been talking about something much more trivial.

"What about you? What keeps you awake?"

Rori shook his head slowly. He knew she wanted to redirect the conversation, so he went with it. "Stupid things. Wondering what the next day will bring. Wondering how many people there are left alive. And then really, really stupid things. Like what if I never end up taking my A Levels? And when am I going to be able to get a haircut?"

Heidi frowned at Rori for a minute before spluttering into laughter. It was such an infectious sound that Rori began to laugh as well. Because he knew he was ridiculous. He knew his anxieties made no sense. And now, as he spoke them aloud, he realized just how silly it was to have those worries on his mind.

"Fucking hell, Rori. Haircuts, of all things?"

Rori grinned and ran a hand through his hair, ruffling up the blonde waves. "I've got to keep myself looking good. Otherwise, how will the rotters know I'm the catch of the day?"

Heidi snorted again and the pair of them descended back into giggles. It felt good to laugh. It felt like releasing all of the bad that had pent up inside him. And when Heidi laughed, she seemed so much less guarded. Like she wasn't keeping up appearances, acting a clown to cover her own insecurities. For a moment, she looked happy, if only briefly. She shook her head at him.

"Oh, Rori," Heidi wheezed, wiping tears from her eyes. "I'm so glad I've got you with me through all this."

Luke was standing in the middle of the fields. The sun was close to setting, and he knew it would soon be dangerous to be out in the open, like Gemma had been the night that she died. But for now, he could survey the land with a clear line of sight.

He knew they had to start thinking about their future there. They couldn't keep living from day to day. That's why he'd been so keen to ration their foods, to keep stock of what they had and figure out how long it would be before they ran out. Now, they had a little more to keep them going, thanks to their trip off of the farm a few days prior. The trip he'd dreaded so much had proved to be very important to their supplies.

But it wouldn't be enough to last them through the winter. And when the days started to get shorter, when the fields became barren and bare, they would start to feel it. Luke looked out over the land and knew that things would have to change in order for them to survive.

"What are you doing?"

Luke jolted at the sound of someone speaking to him. He hadn't heard anyone approach, and when he turned to see Hannah looking up at him, he felt even more surprised. Hannah gazed at him expectantly with her intelligent eyes, her hands clasped behind her back. It was the first time she had ventured out of the house in a while, and Luke wondered whether Ginge knew she was out there alone.

"It's okay. I asked her if I could go for a walk," Hannah said, reading Luke's mind. "She said she'd watch me from the house. She thinks I should get used to taking care of myself a little more."

Luke knew why Ginge was keen to make Hannah grow up a little. The unspoken fact was that if something happened to Ginge, to the others, then Hannah would have to learn how to survive alone. She was too young still to be faced with such things, but too old to be exempt. Still, in some ways, she seemed to be better prepared than Cara. The fact that she was brave enough to leave the house - after all the horrors her young eyes had seen - shocked Luke.

"I see," Luke said stiffly. He didn't really know how to talk to the younger girl. People his own age were enough to baffle him sometimes, but kids were a mystery to him. Especially kids like Hannah, who seemed wise beyond their age.

"What are you doing?" Hannah repeated. Luke shoved his hands into the pockets of his hoodie, surveying the land once more.

"I'm wondering how best to defend this place," Luke said honestly. He didn't have the patience to mollycoddle Hannah too much, especially if Ginge was trying to get her used to the new world that had dawned on them. "There's a lot of land to cover. We want to ensure that the rotters don't get close enough to harm us. Ideally, we want to stop them from getting onto our land at all."

Hannah stood beside Luke and copied his stance, her small hands buried in the pockets of her pinafore dress. She frowned deeply, like she was concentrating hard.

And then she said something strange.

"You should just dig a big pit."

Luke blinked at her. "What?"

Hannah looked up at him seriously. "You should make a big pit all around the farm. And then If anything tries to get close, it just gets stuck in the pit. The monsters aren't very smart, are they? Maybe they won't be able to get out."

It was a simple yet surprisingly good idea, Luke thought. In theory, at least. In practice, they'd have to dig a pit miles wide to cover all of their land. But he thought maybe she might be onto something.

"I suppose that could work on a small scale…a deep pit just around the house. Like a moat without any water. That's how castles used to protect themselves from invasion…"

"I know. I read about it in history," Hannah said.

"Of course you did," Luke said. Perhaps he'd underestimated the child beside him. She was clearly smart, and creative. Maybe that's what he was missing. He knew how to lean into logic, but his ideas were too small for what they were facing.

Maybe the kid would be a useful asset to the farm.

He began to think harder about the idea. The trench would be perfect for slowing down the rotters, for trapping them in place and preparing them for slaughter. If they dug it deep enough, they'd certainly have the high ground, in a literal sense. They could take care of the rotters from a distance and minimize the possibility of harming themselves. They might even be able to relax a little. So long as they checked the pits a few times a day and dealt with the immediate threat, they might not even need to keep constant watch. The thought was so relieving to Luke that he felt his shoulders dip a little. For the first time in days, he felt like they were about to get a handle on the new era they'd all entered. All because of one kid and the ideas captured in her imagination.

"Any other bright ideas?" Luke asked. Hannah blinked several times.

"I'll let you know when they come to me."

Luke almost laughed. He was starting to like the kid. After the chaos of the past few days, he felt like she was one of the few people on the farm who would listen to him without question. He'd grown tired of all of the debates, of the democracy, of the arguing amongst themselves. He was tired of people never agreeing with his thoughts, taking his ideas and trampling all over them.

Perhaps he had found himself an ally.

In the silence that fell between them, a loud moan could be heard, echoing over the empty fields from the distance. Hannah's head snapped up at the noise, and she froze, squinting through the darkness to the surrounding fields.

"What was that?" she asked Luke, her voice full of uncertainty. Luke swallowed nervously. He was no good with kids usually, and he certainly didn't sign up to babysit this one if things turned hairy. He grabbed his knife from his belt, ready for anything.

"Probably just the wind," he lied. Somewhere out there, somewhere not too far away, there was a rotter lurking. At first, he couldn't make anything out against the inky blackness of the sky.

Then he saw them.

Writhing, moaning and dragging their feet behind them in a half-hearted shuffle came an army of rotters over the fields. They were perhaps a couple of hundred meters away from them, but they were there all the same, and approaching the farm with a relentless energy fuelled by their hunger.

"What is it?" Hannah asked, tugging on Luke's sleeve urgently. He bent down beside her and put his hands on her shoulders.

"Listen to me. You need to go to the house and find your sister. Tell her that everyone needs to get out here, and they need to be armed. Then go into the attic with your brother and stay there. Do you understand?"

Hannah nodded quietly. It was clear she understood the urgency of the situation, but she didn't seem panicked. She turned back to the house and broke out into a run, her small arms and legs propelling her forward. Luke straightened up again, feeling like the breath had been knocked out of his lungs.

He hadn't imagined it. It was like a storm of them were descending on the farm. So many of them he couldn't begin to count. He thought back to the roadblock in town. He guessed the rotters had changed their target.

And now the target was them.

At an estimate, Luke guessed that they would be on the farm in less than an hour. They had a little time to prepare. They had to stop the rotters from getting too close to the farm if they could. But he feared that their preparation would be far from enough to keep them alive.

Not when the horde arrived.

Epilogue

Ross would do anything to stay alive.

And that was why, three days earlier, he'd pushed his closest friend directly into the oncoming herd of rotters back at the college. They'd become trapped in a classroom, just the two of them. Everyone else they'd known was dead or gone, and the horde had finally caught up to them.

He'd paused for a moment to watch the betrayal cross Jamie's face, before his emotional hurt became physical. Then, when the rotters began to tear off chunks of Jamie, Ross finally ran away.

It was him or me, Ross told himself, his heart racing almost as fast as his feet. *It was him or me...*

And it had to be him.

He didn't regret it. Why should he? The horde had forced their way past their barricades, broken down all of their defenses, promised death to them as they reached out with dirty fingernails and bloodied hands. They'd cut Ross and Jamie off at a dead end. Jamie had thought they would die side by side, but where was the sense in that? Why should they both die when one of them could survive?

Jamie had been ready to die, and that was why he had to be the one to go.

Ross was stronger. He knew how high the stakes for survival were set.

And he had a new rule; to always be surrounded by easier targets.

He'd been alone afterwards, but he'd survived. He'd made it out of the college and started to run for his life. Running down the empty streets, his armpits stained with sweat and his face dripping with Jamie's blood, he promised himself that he wouldn't let his friend be a sacrifice for nothing.

He ran until he thought he would collapse. He ran until his muscles felt like they were being torn apart. He slept a little, but mostly he ran, because running was the only thing he knew now. It was his first line of defense.

And it had paid off. Ross allowed himself a smug smile as he settled down in the high school cafeteria. Now he had found a new safe haven. This was his fresh start. He had food, electricity, weapons and a group of gullible children he could manipulate to keep him safe. It had been surprisingly easy to take the school from those older kids, the ones who had fled at the first sign of trouble. He was glad of it. This would be the start of his own empire, where he was on top. He'd survive at all costs. He'd be ruthless if he had to be. He'd show them all how powerful he was.

Even if he had to kill to get there.

Coming Soon…

Book 3: Chaos

About the Authors

HAYLEY ANDERTON is a full time ghostwriter and the author of the YA LGBT romance novel, Double Bluff. When she's not writing she loves to bake and hang out with her cat. She would 100% never survive the zombie apocalypse.

Hayley's dystopian thriller, The Last Girls on Earth, is now available to pre-order on Amazon. For editing services and business enquiries, she can be contacted at hayleyandertonbusiness@gmail.com.

Instagram: @handerton96
Twitter: @handerton96
Wattpad: @hazzer123

LAURA SWIFT is a math graduate and business consultant, which she insists is more exciting than it sounds. She enjoys a busy city life in Manchester and you'll often find her at her local pub on a Friday night. In her spare time, Laura loves nothing more than exploring new places and hanging out with her book club.

If you loved this book, don't forget to leave a review on Amazon and Goodreads!

The original Apocalypse series that we wrote for fun almost ten years ago can be found on Wattpad!

Printed in Great Britain
by Amazon